POWER PLAY

G.A.HAUSER

G. A. HAUSER

POWER PLAY

Copyright © G.A. Hauser, 2014

Cover design by Mark Richfield

ISBN Trade paperback: 978-1500265434

© The G.A. Hauser Collection LLC

First The G.A. Hauser Collection LLC publication:
July 2014

Chapter 1

"Running for office is always ugly with tons of mudslinging, but that doesn't mean I have to be on the front page of every newspaper and the victim of every tweet."

"Look, David, as your chief of staff, and campaign advisor, I think you have to just man up. You can deny the allegations but in my experience the voters would prefer an honest man who screwed up, to a liar."

Talking to his advisor on speaker-phone, Senator David Asher tapped his pen on his desk nervously. The timing of this incident was too coincidental. As he peered around his office in the nation's capital, he had imagined different things for his future. "I agree, Eric, but I already came clean two years ago that the reason Lydia and I are divorced is because I'm gay. You said the fallout would be worse, but it wasn't." David stopped his frantic pen tapping and swiveled in the chair. "I stepped up, like you told me to. Which I agreed with. I told the American public the reason for my leaving Lydia was because I can no longer deny my sexual orientation." David heard Eric Sutten, his chief of staff and close friend, gearing up for a comment and said over him, "It's not like my children are babies. Both of them are in college, Eric. Even Lydia is standing by me. She is not slandering me, not threatening to write tell-all books. She has been supportive and professional."

"Well, you and Lydia have been more like best friends for twenty years than husband and wife. It's no secret she had affairs. With your blessing, I may add."

"True. She's an amazing woman. She deserved better than me." David rubbed his eyes, then ran his hand through his hair. "You really expect me to fess up to these allegations? I did not do anything wrong."

"David, someone hacked into your private emails."

"Fuck." David knew being an out gay democrat with hopes of running for president was bad enough, but this? A scandal? One he wasn't even guilty of? Who was trying to sabotage him?

"Let me think about it." David blew out a loud breath.

"Don't take long. The longer you wait, the guiltier you appear."

David hung up the desk phone by pushing a button and rocked in his leather chair. He picked up his personal smart-phone and scanned through the apps. Seeing the tweets becoming more aggressive and accusing, David felt a lump in his throat.

Forty-seven, divorced, two kids…he thought he was doing the right thing. The political climate had changed; out gay men and women were being elected at every level of government. The far right weren't even using their sexuality to battle them on public debates and endorsements any longer. If they did the backlash from the majority was brutal.

So someone in the opposing party had somehow hacked into his personal emails and became privy to a conversation. A *private conversation*, David had with a younger man he had met.

David reread the email which had now been made public.

It didn't matter if he deleted it, it was already going viral on all the social networks.

Yes, he thought the French model Deon Gael, was handsome. Yes, he knew the man was gay and only twenty-nine. Yes, he had exchanged a little flirty conversation with him at the fashion show fundraising event.

Deon Gael, a spectacular runway model born in Paris, working primarily in New York, modeled for all the best French designers; Oleg Casini, Christian Dior... and...yes, they hit it off.

After the fashion show it was Deon who approached David, shaking his hand and introducing himself. Well, that accent, the fabulous looks and body of Deon, what man would not have been swept up in the chance of romance?

But of course, being aware the mixer was overflowing with reporters, competitors, and people who simply loved gossip, all he had done was given Deon his business card and mentioned coffee or a drink.

They didn't blow each other in the men's room.

And the email? One line from Deon. '*So, when shall we meet?*'

Suddenly David was the 'wild outside candidate' who wanted one-night rendezvous with fabulous French models.

Well, of course he did. But that didn't mean he would jeopardize his campaign or reputation just because he wanted to sip a cocktail with Deon.

But on the other hand.

Why couldn't he?

David was legally divorced, out publically, and Deon was single and free to do as he liked.

Now he had everyone on his staff; the legislative director, his press secretary, his legislative correspondent, all his underlings right down to his staff assistant, telling him 'no'. Don't have drinks with Deon.

David rocked in his leather chair and for the life of him could not figure out why he and Deon could not be seen together, as friends, having a drink or a cup of coffee.

Yes, David was slightly older but Deon was nearly thirty, and David felt and looked like he was in his mid-thirties. Nothing made sense. It was not sneaking. It was not unsavory. Deon was not a porn star with a reputation as a player. The man was single and free, dating as he wished, but David had done his research. Deon Gael was a professional, in everything he did in life.

David stopped reading the tweets, since nothing annoyed him more than the social networks' horrific influence on the madness of society.

David defiantly removed Deon's contact number from his wallet and called him.

"Hello?"

That thick French accent sent the hairs rising on the back of David's neck.

"Mr Gael," David said, smiling, "It's Senator Asher."

"*Ahhh*, Senator Asher, so good to hear your voice. I thought with all the noise of the press…"

"Well, that's what I wanted to chat with you about." David felt his body go into heat thinking about this man. He rocked gently in his chair and tapped the pen again on the desk. "I'm divorced. I am an out gay man. You are single. And well, I simply don't know why two men can't have a drink together?"

"We are grown-ups, yes?"

"Yes."

"I find you attractive, you find me attractive."

David felt his skin rush with chills and his cheeks go warm. "Yes."

"Do we care? This we have to ask. What harm will come? To me? None. To you?…how you say…*êtes-vous inquiet*?"

"I don't know what you asked."

"*Uhhh…*"

David heard Deon struggling to find the right words, so David asked, "Are you asking if I'm worried?"

"Yes. Worry. Have fear."

"Well, that's what I am trying to figure out. Why should I be afraid to be seen with a handsome model? I'm no longer married, and I am a gay man."

"Senator. Yes? U.S. politics…Is all crazy."

David smiled. "True. You won't get an argument from me."

A tap came to his door and his staff assistant, Terry Windham, poked his head in. Seeing David was on the phone, Terry pointed to his own wristwatch, as if reminding David he had an appointment.

David nodded, straightened his tie and asked, "Can I have one of my cars pick you up?"

"Of course!"

"Good. We can decide what to do together. I mean, drinks or dinner." David peeked at Terry who was obviously listening.

"Yes, *à quelle heure*?…What time?"

"Eight?"

"Eight. See you then."

David hung up, smiling.

Terry approached the desk, shaking his head. "No you didn't." He wagged his finger.

David stood, buttoning his jacket. "Terry, we are big boys, both capable of seeing each other without breaking a law, moral or otherwise."

"Oh no, David. Someone is out to sabotage your chances at the White House in the next election."

"Terry…" David put his arm around Terry's shoulder, a man who happened to be gay as well. He walked to the door of his large office with him. "I'm divorced. Lydia is fine with it, supported me coming out, I am just having a drink…."

Terry gave David a warning glance.

8

"Uh uh!" David held up his finger. "A drink, maybe a few appetizers... with a friend."

"He's not a friend. He's a French runway model. Who, may I add, Mr Senator, is only twenty-nine."

"Precisely. Twenty-nine, not fourteen." David coaxed Terry into the hall.

"Sir, the press will go crazy. The tweets are already..."

"Terry." David slowed them down as they began to approach a crowd waiting for David in the hallway. "I am allowed to be a man as well as a public figure."

"Oh my God. Eric will kill me, he'll have a cow."

"You tell my chief of staff to have a cow at me, not you." David smiled at the group he was meeting with. Out of the side of his mouth he asked Terry, "Who are they again?"

"The Farmers League against labeling state crops with GMO."

"Damn." David brightened up and reached out his hand to greet them. "Yes, so nice to speak with you."

"Senator, we have concerns."

"Of course."

His press secretary, Leona Whitman, came to his side. "This way, ladies and gentlemen. The senator will be happy to answer your questions, and seek your endorsement for the upcoming primary."

"Senator, now that you have declared your intentions to run for office at the White House, how are you handling the degrading comments about you on the social media?"

David gave Terry and Leona a quizzical look since this was supposed to be about farmers and the labeling of food. "I'm afraid we'll have to save those questions for another time. Just take a seat and relax." He smiled and waved towards a conference room. As they entered, David stopped Leona and asked, "What the fuck?"

She shrugged. "You do get, Senator, it's what everyone wants to know." Leona rolled her eyes. "Even corn-growers."

Terry smirked, "Corn-holers."

David nudged them both inside the conference room with him and closed the door.

~

Deon sipped strong coffee in his hotel room, reading the newspaper. In French someone called for him and tapped his door. Deon stood and opened it, seeing one of the staff members of his modeling agency, a young woman named Clair. She was his personal assistant.

"I hope you are not following the mess on twitter," she said quickly in French, "Did you have an affair with a US senator?"

Deon gestured for her to step in, and they stood together by the door. "Not yet. No. We spoke at the dinner last night. He is charming. Am I interested, yes, but we haven't so much as exchanged anything but a handshake."

"*Mon Dieu*, they do anything to make a scandal."

Deon shrugged. "It is this way with all public figures." He returned to his couch and coffee.

"So, that is it? All nonsense?"

"So far. Look, Clair, Senator Asher is magnificent. Strikingly handsome, holds himself like a diplomat. I am not out for his ruin. But we have mutual sexual attraction. So?" He shrugged and sipped from his cup.

Still speaking in French, Clair looked frantic. "You want to embroil yourself in an American scandal?"

"What scandal?" Deon threw up his free hand. "He is divorced, he is out as a gay man! What scandal?"

"Then why this? Hmm?" She held her phone and showed him the tweets that were scrolling up and down it.

He brushed them aside. "Jealousy. Who listens to rubbish?"

Clair tapped her toe and folded her arms.

"What?" Deon admonished her. "I have spare time here. Yes, I have a week on the runway floor, so? I like him. He speaks to me as if I have a brain. So, go." He waved her off. "His company is delightful."

"You can ruin you and ruin him."

He set the cup down in anger. "This I cannot see." He stood up and stared down at her. "How? Hmm? Two men, two adults. No conflict. None. You make it sound as if we are hiding. Sneaking. He is single now, I am single. We have coffee? A chat…"

"Just be careful. You don't live here. You have no idea how hungry Americans are for scandal. They don't care if you are single, he is *divorced*!" she said loudly. "Not single, and he is running for the highest seat in their political office."

Deon was exasperated. "We are two gay men who find mutual attraction and interests. What business is it of anyone?"

She held the phone in front of his face. "Shall I read them to you?"

He pushed her hand away. "Get that out away from me. You will have me for my work tomorrow night. My time until then? Whose is it?"

Clair muttered to herself in anger as she walked to the door of the hotel. Then before she left she said, "I have seen these bad political scandals before. You and this man, whom you think is so wise, so sophisticated. You are both fooling yourselves. You will crumble like a house of cards here."

"Doing what?" Deon threw up his hands. "Having a cocktail? A nibble of food?"

"You know what I mean."

"I am free to see anyone. This country and my own? Yes?"

"Be careful!"

"Oh! Leave. You are giving me a headache!"

Clair left and Deon sat down on the chair trying to recover from her warning. He peeked at his phone and picked it up.

Against his better judgment he read the tweets, which were coming now both from his own country and the USA.

He threw down the phone in anger. "Two men? Two men cannot socialize?"

Deon rested length-wise on the couch and tried to close his eyes. The moment he was introduced to David he thought he was exquisite. His full head of hair, touched with silver at the temples, trim tall, with dark brown eyes.

The man knew everything, so worldly, so savvy to the international well-being of the earth, and the people who inhabited it.

Deon was sick of being treated like a dumb model. He was far from it. He had come from wealth, educated in the finest schools, and spoke several languages. But modeling is where he ended up. Why? He didn't know.

But his face and body became his fame and fortune, so? For now, until he aged, he could capitalize on it and he simply would. He was not about to marry, to find a man to have a commitment, not now, not while he traveled and worked hard. And what was so wrong with someone as wonderful as a senator having him for dinner?

"Nothing." He made a noise of disgust in his throat and let go his anger.

~

"What room is he staying in?"

"Room twenty-thirteen."

The young man adjusted the collar of his white shirt and asked, "Do I look like I'm from room service?"

His friend laughed and made sure his collar was straight and his dark suit jacket lint free. "Perfect."

The young man held a bucket of ice which contained an expensive bottle of champagne and he wore white gloves. "Cool. See ya."

"You are so bad!"

"Oh, this is just the beginning." The young man gave his friend a smirk. "Let me go before someone sees me."

His friend left so he took the back stairs instead of the elevator and then before he knocked he made sure he stood straight and proper, and the bucket of champagne appeared presentable. He tapped the door.

It took a moment, but it opened.

"Yes?" Deon Gael answered, looking so gorgeous, the young man tried not to drool.

"A gift, sir, from the hotel." The young man gestured to the champagne.

"Oh? For what?" Deon opened the door wider, allowing the young man inside his suite.

"I'm not sure. But I was told to tell you, it's from an admirer." The young man spotted a counter near a sink and microwave and placed the cold bucket on it.

"Oh? Is there a card?" Deon inspected the champagne.

"I don't know." The young man pretended to look with him. "Huh. I guess it may have fallen. I'm sorry."

"No need." Deon smiled and read the label of the bottle. "Is very expensive taste."

"Shall I open it, sir?"

"Perhaps I shall save it? Hmm? For later?"

The young man's smile began to turn into a frown. "But, it's perfectly chilled." The young man looked in the cupboards and removed two fluted glasses from the well-stocked bar area.

"Two?" Deon laughed as he gave the man a closer inspection.

The young man smiled and opened the cork with a pop. He held the champagne over the sink as it overflowed, then poured two glasses. Once he had, the young man held his up and gave Deon a sensual smile. "What if I were to tell you, I am the admirer."

Deon sipped the champagne. "I am very flattered."

The young man tapped Deon's glass and they both tasted it.

"You work here?" Deon pointed to the hall, as if indicating the hotel.

"Shh. No." The young man put his finger to his lips. "I just was dying to meet you. I didn't think I could unless I planned to do it this way."

Deon blinked in surprise. "I am still flattered, and yet slightly nervous."

"Oh, don't worry." The young man shook his head and held up his hand. "I'm not a stalker or anything. I mean, I won't bother you."

Deon sipped more of the champagne. "It is very good. You pick this out yourself?"

"I did. I…" He removed his white gloves slowly. "Have very good taste." He gave Deon a sexy smile. "In all things."

"I see." Deon smiled back. "Now, I am knowing why you come."

"Do you find me attractive?" The young man removed the jacket and held out his arms.

"You are not unattractive. Yes?" Deon sipped more champagne.

"Are you involved with someone?"

"No. No one. Solo. Uh, how you say? Only."

The young man nodded. "Good. I mean. I know you like men. I was hoping you liked me."

"I never had someone so forward as to pull a charade." Deon's blue eyes glimmered, and young man could tell how he had appealed to this model's ego.

"I know. It makes me look kind of crazy. But I'm not. I tried to get closer to you at the dinner, but wow, you were swamped with admirers."

"Yes. As you say. Swamped. It is hard to meet for real anyone to speak with."

The young man topped off Deon's glass. "So, um…I know this sounds really crazy but, do you want to have sex?"

Deon choked on the sip of champagne and sprayed it out of his mouth, coughing.

"Hmm." The young man tapped his chin. "I guess that's a no?"

"Sex? A man dresses as a server, comes to my door to give me gift, and now he asks for sex." Deon laughed and cleared his throat. "Yes, that is more what I am used to."

"I'll bet. I mean. Wow." The young man gestured to Deon. "You're…well…you're the most amazing man I have ever seen. I mean, in person."

"How old? Hmm? How is your age?"

"Twenty-three." The young man lied and stepped slightly closer to Deon. "I swear, I won't tell a soul. I'll keep it between me and you."

"What is it you keep, that is my curiosity?" Deon finished the champagne and set down the glass.

The young man knelt down on the floor and stared at Deon's crotch. "I give great blowjobs."

"Twenty-three? Yet went to so much trouble just for the pleasure of sucking my dick?" Deon put his hands on his hips. "You want me this badly?"

"Oh, you have no idea." The young man stared at Deon's crotch.

After a moment, Deon laughed. "You make it hard to refuse. I feel I owe, so much cost for champagne."

He looked up at Deon's eyes. "Was that a yes?"

"So, just you want to taste me? That is why you went through all this trouble?"

"Yes. Wow. I'd do anything you wanted. I mean, while you're here? In town? If you just want to fuck someone?"

"Now you offer me your services as my personal sex man. Hmm, this keeps getting deeper." Deon rubbed his jaw. "You say it mean nothing, but sex, well, to me, sex mean everything."

The young man sat on his heels. "It's cool. I figured I'd give it a shot. I won't stalk you, man. I promise."

Deon reached out his hand.

The young man was hauled to his feet.

Just as he expected to be shown the door, Deon led him to his bedroom. "Oh yes!" The young man pumped his fist.

"You can suck. Is good?" Deon lowered his trousers and briefs, and sat on the bed.

"Man! Yes!" The young man dropped to his knees and went for Deon's cock. He sucked it deeply while it was soft, inhaling expensive cologne and seeing how well-groomed Deon's pubic hair was. Perfection, like everything about him.

Deon caressed the young man's hair and moaned softly. "You suck very well. I can tell you do this many times before."

"Mm." The young man closed his eyes and swooned. He sucked Deon, nudging him to lie back on the bed and relax.

Then as Deon did, allowing him to enjoy himself, and play, the young man removed his phone from his pocket and began taking video of the act.

The young man gripped Deon's cock in one hand, making Deon moan and finally come. Deon, relaxed, his legs spread, and recuperated as the young man took a few more secret photos, and then pocketed his smart-phone.

He stood up and stared down at the beautiful model. "Wow. I can't believe you let me do that. I mean, you don't even know me."

"I no usual do this. But…It was nice. Yes?" Deon sat up, and drew his clothing up his body. "I walk you out."

"It's okay."

"I insist." Deon fastened his pants and the young man headed to the door of the hotel room looking back at the opulence and spacious rooms.

"Enjoy the champagne." The young man smiled.

"Yes. I will. Thank you. I do not know your name."

"No. You don't." The young man smirked and left. As he walked down the hall he reviewed the video he had taken and congratulated himself with a fist in the air and a silent cheer. He dialed and said, "Phase one, complete."

Chapter 2

David straightened his tie in the mirror and heard his phone ring. He glanced at it and could tell it was his ex-wife. He picked it up and said, "What's up, Lydia?"

"I'm just seeing how you are holding up. The news is making me sick."

"I'm fine. Thanks. But its not the first time the media has tried to crush me. I seem to bounce back all right."

"I'm here. I mean it, David. I'm a strong supporter of same sex rights and if you want me by your side through any of this, just ask."

David smiled. "You are an amazing woman. I'm a very lucky man."

"You're a good man. An honest one."

One of his aides made a motion for David to hurry.

"Thanks, Lydia. I may just take you up on that as the campaign heats up."

"I don't get it, David. There are so many real issues to discuss, why is sexuality between two consenting adults one of them?"

"You do realize how many discussions you and I have had over this topic? I don't know the answer." David thanked his aide for handing him his suit jacket.

"Well, until it blows over, you have me. Do you want me to call your press secretary? Make a statement that you are a free man and can do as he pleases?"

"Not yet. I think this is just a blip. You know. A slow news day." He held the phone as his assistant helped him put the jacket on. "I'm going out for a drink tonight with Deon."

"You know I have no objections, but considering the crazy press you two are getting, are you sure that's wise?"

"I'm never sure. But not going out with him? Having hateful people make decisions in my personal life?" David nodded 'thank you' to his aide and was led out the door to a line of black sedans and a security escort.

"I agree to a certain extent, David, but do keep in mind your career."

David halted in his tracks. "What have I done?" He threw up one hand in frustration. "I'm a man, Lydia. I have needs outside work."

"I know. I just worry."

"And I love you for it. Gotta go." He disconnected his call and pocketed the phone.

"First limo, sir, behind the police escort."

"Seems a bit much for drinks with a friend." David frowned.

"Eric Sutten's orders. He said until the media frenzy calms down he wants you protected."

"My chief of staff is wasting taxpayer money. If he thinks that's good publicity he and Leona need to have a sit down with me."

"Mr Sutten hired a private service, sir. This is not funded by the state."

"Fine." David sat in the back of the sedan and tried to relax.

His safety and well being wasn't always this threatened. But since he had become high profile with many interviews on television; including the comedy network and late night host's hot topic, about being out, being in a 'happy divorce', David had become some kind of folk hero.

A place he was not thrilled to be in. He wanted to help people, do the right thing, but there were so many maniacs and extremist out there, he never knew if Eric was being wise or over-cautious with a caravan of security.

The small procession began moving and it never failed to make everyone on the street stop and stare, wondering which DC dignitary was being carted around.

The hotel was only a few miles away.

David waited, resisting peeking at his phone or messages since lately they were bleak.

The car door was opened and Deon, looking irresistible in his Christian Dior silk suit and black tie, climbed in. Deon appeared overwhelmed and said, "I thought when you say you have a car pick me up..."

"Yes, well. Welcome to my life."

"How you can live so big?" Deon sat back as the car began to move.

"It's not always like this. Between the announcement of my bid to run for president, and the latest tweets to derail it, my chief of staff is paranoid."

"Should he be?"

David sighed. "Who knows?"

"America with its guns...too many crazy people."

"I'm not sure that's what he's afraid of. To be honest I don't know what's going on at the moment."

"We just forget everything and share a drink." Deon put his hand on David's knee.

David met his blue eyes. "Yes. Those are my thoughts exactly." He put his hand on top of Deon's.

Deon smiled and leaned for a kiss, one David did not expect. It was a sweet peck, but lit David on fire. He squeezed Deon's hand tightly. "You'll be a hard man to resist, my friend."

"Who are we resisting for?"

As they drove to a fancy restaurant where they could eat privately, David stared out of the tinted window and replied, "I don't know."

He felt Deon try to get his attention. David shook himself out of his thoughts of work and turned in the leather seat to meet Deon's gaze.

"You and I," Deon began touching his own chest and then indicating David, "We do not make commitment. No. We are free men. Am I correct?"

"Yes."

"Then..." Deon struggled with the words as if trying to translate first in his head. "So, where is worry from? They can no say we cheat. I have no lover, you have divorce. They can say nothing about men with men. I am out comfortable, you are out comfortable."

David nodded, loving staring at Deon. But he appreciated Deon as a man of the world, an intellectual, not just a pretty face.

"What can they do? Hmm?" Deon shrugged. "Adults, consenting, and a world where things change in so many good ways. Men can marry men, women can marry women...Life is good."

David reached behind Deon's neck and drew him to his mouth. The kiss was electric and Deon's whimpers were so sexy David fought to control himself.

When the car stopped, so did he. He sat back and caught his breath.

Deon stared at him with what appeared to be both a mixture of sexual desire and surprise. "I think you are man of so many textures."

"You mean layers?" David chuckled. "I hope."

The back door was opened for them.

"Yes. Layer. What does texture mean?"

David touched the fabric of Deon's suit jacket.

Deon blushed. "My English. I try well, but not always succeed."

"You do succeed." David gestured for Deon to exit the car. As he did, David got a good look at his ass, and knew getting this man into bed was going to take tact, patience, and time.

They were shown to a dimly lit restaurant and several secret service-type bodyguards were communicating through earpieces as the two men entered and were shown to a private dining area in back.

They were seated by a host, and offered champagne and cocktails.

David asked, as he unbuttoned his jacket and sat down across from Deon, "Should I order us a bottle of champagne?"

"No." Deon sat comfortably and thanked the host for the menu. "Strangely, someone brought a bottle to my room."

"Oh?" David tried not to be jealous. "An admirer?"

"Yes. So it seems. You must get many. Yes?"

David tried to take the comment without a reaction. "That's very flattering. What would you like?"

"A martini or red wine? Is all good. I am not a picky drinker. Eater, *oui*, but, as long as the alcohol is of good quality..." He winked.

David gestured to a serving staff member who was waiting for their order. "I would like a dirty martini. Two?" David asked Deon.

"Yes. Perfect." Deon nodded.

A waiter placed Deon's napkin on his lap for him, as water was poured from bottles by a second server.

Deon looked around.

The restaurant staff was awaiting orders, as well as David's personnel and security.

"This is what you call a private evening?"

David spotted Deon's appraisal of the situation, reading his thoughts before he spoke them. "I couldn't agree more." He craned his finger to one of his own men. The man leaned down.

"Can you guys give us some space? This is ridiculous. If Eric has an issue with it, he can speak to me…tomorrow. If I see any of you lurking, I'll ask you to wait outside."

"Yes, sir." The security officer appeared conflicted, and David knew Eric most likely said, 'you lose sight of this man and you'll be fired'. But Eric was not the man in charge. He was.

Once his own security cleared out, Deon appeared less preoccupied.

"Are you hungry?" David asked.

"Yes, actually. I am." Deon read the menu.

Their martinis were brought to the table, and once they were set down, the server asked, "May I make a few suggestions?"

Deon immediately lowered the menu to listen.

As a few fresh selections were noted, David stared at Deon's profile, already imagining them naked and playing, but men like Deon, and for the sake of his own reputation, had to move carefully.

But it didn't stop his imagination from taking wing.

~

Once Deon chose the black truffle appetizer and a main course of filet mignon, he relaxed and stared at this handsome senator. He certainly knew enough about American politics that he may be seated besides the next U.S. President. Did it influence him? Perhaps. Maybe the same way his own sexuality and looks influenced a man of power to ask him for dinner, or wasn't it drinks? It was meaningless, here they were, together.

In their worlds, power was attained in different ways. Deon attained his from being a handsome man, who was tall, slender, and had the 'look' all the French fashion designers craved. So Deon's power was being in-demand. What he wore, sold, and drew the attention of buyers for large retail chain stores. And in his game, money and how much of it could be made, and who could sell the most, won.

G. A. HAUSER

As Deon sipped the martini, he wondered if perhaps he and David were not very different types of men. Both were alpha, powerful men, wealthy, in positions at the top of their professional food chain.

But Deon was not so headstrong to believe the mighty could not fall.

He'd seen everything; from his peers getting eating disorders, to becoming so insecure about their looks they were led down the path of drugs to poverty and self-destruction.

Deon had neither a drug habit nor an eating disorder. Though he could have been, he was no prima dona. He wanted to be easy to get along with. Being kind brought more work. Throwing tantrums got you banned.

Once David gave his order to the waiter, and they were finally left alone in a wonderful curtained space that felt both cozy and exotic, Deon set his drink down and turned on the rounded bench seat they were sharing to face him. "So, tell me about David Asher the man, not the politician."

David smiled shyly and Deon loved the dimples in his cheeks. The smile made David radiant.

"I used to have time for hobbies." David sipped his drink and then, he too, turned on the soft seat so their knees nearly touched. "When I could indulge in frivolity, I played tennis, enjoyed golfing…"

Deon grew lost in David's dark eyes, the arch of his eyebrows and the hollow under his high cheekbones. His voice was deep, commanding, as a man of his power should be. Coming out as a gay man to the public had done nothing to weaken the strength of this individual.

David was pure masculinity in his every move and gesture. A trait Deon was incredibly attracted to. In modeling the men were a veritable rainbow from macho to androgynous.

Deon stayed quiet, giving David a slight nod to continue.

David paused thoughtfully and said, "I also enjoy creative arts. I love to paint, to write…"

"Do you?" Deon grew excited. "Painting?"

"Not so much anymore." David appeared modest and Deon loved it.

"And what style do you write?"

"Actually…" David scooted slightly closer placing his hand behind Deon on the soft seat. "Memoirs. Hopefully documenting the first out gay man's journey into the White House."

"I would read this book." Deon sipped the martini, giving David a slightly flirty smile. "Will I get my own chapter?"

Hearing David laugh delighted Deon.

They were interrupted when a server brought their appetizers. Both men sat facing the table, moving away as if they had not been touching, nearly about to kiss.

"Thank you." David smiled at the waiter.

"Your main course will be out shortly."

"No rush." David glanced back at Deon.

Deon did not react, only smiled to himself. He tasted the appetizer and enjoyed it. "You must try." He used his own fork and fed David a sample.

"That is good. Here, try this." David removed a small manila clam from its shell and fed it to Deon.

"Mm. Splendid. Yes."

"We can share." David moved his plate closer and his body as well, so they were almost touching. They split the appetizers and made noises indicating how good it was.

"So," Deon dabbed his lip with his cloth napkin, "I read only good about how your ex-wife has taken this change."

David sipped his water first, then nodded. "Yes. She and I had long talks before we divorced, trying to decide how to make it seamless and not a press field day."

"She…she is not upset? No?"

"No." David glanced around first as if making sure they could not be overheard, then spoke softly, "She and I have had an agreement for many years. She was free to do as she liked. She…she knew years ago of my preference."

"Oh?" Deon was surprised.

"But, twenty years ago, politics was not ready for someone like me. Now, they are. So, we did enjoy a nice life, raised two children, and now with the new open-minded world, she can finally be free to follow her heart, and…" David met Deon's gaze. "I can follow mine. Without so much fuss or repercussions."

"But…the twitter?" Deon became confused.

"That isn't about my candidacy or my sexual orientation. I think, to be honest, it's just a nasty ploy to derail me. I'm ahead in the polls, and well, dirty-business is politics' middle name."

"So…" Deon finished his appetizer and wiped his lips with his napkin, and then held his martini. "So, the mass media is used as a weapon now. Like swords and bullets in war."

"The pen has always been mightier than the sword, and in politics, this is very true."

Deon nodded, thinking. "Is seems cruel. You know? To take a man; an intelligent one, to place him in position to defend."

"I'm used to it. I suppose in some ways I have been battling for what I want all my life." David pushed his plate of empty clam shells aside and touched Deon's leg. "What about you?"

Deon waved him off dismissively. "Gay in fashion? Who is not gay in fashion?"

"So, you have managed to steer clear of scandal?"

"What scandal can they come of me?" Deon asked. "Hmm? My dick is too small?" He shrugged. "So, I have small dick."

David laughed, covering his mouth. A waiter cleared the empty plates and said, "I hope everything was good."

"Yes. Very good." David smiled at Deon.

The warmth from David made Deon excited, yearning to kiss him.

After the waiter cleared the plates and they were left alone, David touched the hair behind Deon's head, right at the nape, giving Deon a chill. He shivered visibly from it and met David's eyes. "I do not know which is more intense for me; your animal sexuality or from power."

As if it didn't matter to David which attribute turned Deon on, he brought Deon's mouth to meet his.

Deon felt the touch of those lips and his entire body reacted. This was no ordinary man. Not in any way. He was not only exquisitely handsome and fit, he was in line for the American throne.

What had Deon to compare David to? Nothing but other models and an occasional admirer…but this? This man of talent and intellect was a true man of the world.

Deon felt the desire to make love to David, to be indiscreet and touch him between his legs. But again, this was no regular man, no fling. He allowed David the pleasure of ending the kiss first and was breathless from it, as they met eyes.

Then as if he could not help himself, David said, "You are spectacular."

Deon tried to sit upright on the soft bench seat and ran his hand over his tie, gaining his self-control. "What I would do with a man like you behind closed doors…" Deon smirked to himself. "Perhaps, one day we shall find out."

David ran his hand from Deon's upper thigh to his knee, and Deon closed his eyes from the excitement this man stirred in him. He was on fire and his cock was thick and throbbing.

A noise outside the curtain seemed to wake each man from their sensual dream. A small parade of dishes proudly presented, were laid on the table and both men had their water refilled.

"Another martini?" the waiter asked, taking the two empty glasses.

Deon touched his hair and said, "I am afraid of what I shall do with two."

David laughed. "I think one is enough."

"Enjoy." The waiter meant the feast, but when David turned and touched Deon's jaw, he said, "I intend to."

Deon's breath caught in his throat and he felt the heat rush over him like a blaze of fire.

As David's touch withdrew and he began tasting the food, Deon gulped the water and tried to control himself. This was not an ordinary man. No. This was a man Deon could lose himself on. And Deon would be the recipient of that powerful man's touch and affection. He could feel the mutual attraction from David easily and tried not to allow himself to get carried away on his fantasies.

He glanced at David who held out a taste of his salmon for Deon. Deon parted his lips and took the bite of food off the fork.

~

Deon's raw sensuality was driving David out of his mind. If he had been in his twenties and in college, he would have already crawled under the table and sucked the man off.

Seeing the expressions of pleasure on Deon's face, how he accepted the food with his teeth from the fork, like there was a wild cat under his calm, pretty, exterior, was making David insane.

They ate silently, only commenting on the food quality, since everything was superb. David began a debate in his mind at what to do at the conclusion of this, 'date'. All the options would be visible to both his own entourage, and the press. So, if he got out of the car and followed Deon to his hotel room, would that be on the front page news and in every tweet? If he took Deon back with him? To his place in DC? Well, that was scandalous.

David had to walk a fine line.

The division of that line was sex. It was fine for him to dine with a beautiful young model. To be seen getting in and out of the cars. But to sleep with him? He knew what would happen. First thing in the morning or even an hour after he had been spotted joining Deon at either residence, his campaign advisor/ chief of staff would be hit with questions regarding how long David and this French stud had fucked. That would not go over well in the polls.

But he was human.

He was a man.

He was a horny man.

A horny man having dinner with an exceptional French model that was not only beautiful but had a brain.

A man who was showing David just how desirable he was in return. Missing out on getting this man in bed would be impossible to forget. Or forgive.

But the political debate began in David's head.

The choice; to act like an ordinary man on a date or a politician who is worried about ruining his candidacy?

One which had already taken a blow by a tweet, a message that was pure bullshit. Yet, even the BS on tweets and blogs, were right until proven wrong. A justice system inverted.

Those nasty rumors, of which he did not want to even hear, were heartless. All David did each day was work and go home, he never dated. But the damage from that tweet, that destructive individual who was of course, untraceable and anonymous ...infuriated David.

The damage inflicted to David's good name had been so horrific, he had to bring the ex-wife with him to meet the press, to pacify his campaign donors, his big guns on the Farm Bureau, the NRA, as well as NAACP, and every other acronym who was trying to lobby for his support.

The solid demographics, the ones he counted on; the gay vote, young peoples' vote, most minorities; liked him. Women liked him...but one wrong move? They'd turn on him as if he'd become rabid. Criminal.

Meanwhile, there is a French model using just his fingertips to touch my thigh.

Kill me now.

David tried to keep eating but the thoughts in his head were driving him crazy. He slowed down and sipped the water.

"Is filling." Deon patted his stomach. "Americans, like to eat, yes?"

"Yes." David laughed.

"Is okay if you excuse? I may use the men's room?"

Just for a moment David wondered if Deon was actually going to throw up, like a model. But hoped that was ridiculous. "Of course."

"You don't go no place." Deon leaned closer teasingly. "I may come back to more kisses. Yes?"

"Yes." They pecked lips and David watched Deon scoot around the table and leave the private room.

He relaxed on the soft sofa-like bench seat and tried to figure it out. Drop Deon off? Get the cavalcade of security vehicles back to his place, then take a cab to the hotel? What? Wearing a ski mask?

David threw his napkin on the table and said, "Fuck me."

~

Deon entered the men's room and washed his hands, then stood at a urinal. He relieved himself and smiled at the thought of being the object of such a powerful man's desires. It was flattery at its finest. And David was magnificent.

He finished and flushed the urinal, then returned to the sink to wash his hands and check his appearance.

"Hello, again."

Deon spun around to see the same young man who had come to his hotel room with the champagne. "What you do here?"

The young man shrugged and touched Deon's tie, as if straightening the knot.

Deon brushed the young man's hands off and said, "You do stalk. You do find me for trouble."

"No. Come on. It's pure coincidence. How would I know you'd be here? Don't be paranoid."

"I am here with very important man. You no come near." Deon wagged his finger.

"Yeah?" The young man leaned closer. "Who are you with? Should I be jealous?"

"You should be gone." Deon made a gesture to the door. "You make me...oh, *Je me sens...*" Deon rubbed his forehead. "Feel wrong. Feel no right."

Appearing unruffled by Deon's nerves, the young man held up his phone as if trying to make Deon see a photo.

"Why you show?" Deon pushed his hand aside. "I no have interest."

"No? I don't see why not. It's you."

"*Moi?* No, you are crazy man."

"I don't know. Sure looks like you getting your cock sucked by me. Huh?"

Deon felt ill and cold sweat began to form on his forehead. He looked at the photos on the phone. "You are sick man."

"Look at how great they are." The young man relaxed against the stall door, using his thumb to move the photos and show Deon as if it were a game. "I won't post them or anything...yet. But. I kind of liked it. You do know I know who you're with, right?"

Deon grew furious and moved within the young man's personal space. "You think I am easy to push? Hmm?"

"Do you think the guy who is going to be the next president of the United States wants people to see what his whore looks like getting a blowjob?"

"Whore?" Deon raised his hand to slap the young man, but the arrogant teen not only appeared to expect it, he smiled.

Holding his phone at an angle to capture everything Deon did, the young man said, "Slap me. Oh, baby. I love it. First slap my face, then my ass. Then fuck me."

Deon pushed the young man's hand down and backed away. "You need help I cannot give you. You know outside door is many men who guard this next president. I need tell them, and you see, you see how quickly you go to jail."

"Why don't you do that?" The youth held up the phone with his thumb over a button. "Then I push this and your and my blowjob party is all over the world. Funny huh? Who has more power? You or me?"

Deon snarled and muttered French expletives, then said, "I blame your parents. They should have placed you over their knee!"

The creep laughed. "If you only knew how funny that really is." The young man looked at the bathroom door. "My buddy won't let anyone in. He's telling people I got sick in here. So?"

Deon backed up, looking at the door.

"You suck mine or I suck yours?"

"Vile pig!" Deon backed up.

"You do realize I am recording you." The young man hit the playback and Deon saw his own face and *'Vile pig!'* was replayed.

"How to deal with this? Hmm? How? You make me want to do things to hurt you." Deon looked back at the door, wondering if he did go, and this punk pushed that button, what would happen to his and David's budding relationship. No doubt, it would be over.

But succumb to the will of some vulgar American teenager?

The young man unzipped his own pants and exposed his cock.

Deon was revolted and looked away.

"Okay, dude. I'm happy to service you again."

"Do not touch me!" Deon held out his hand. "I don't know what this is to do with me. I don't understand." He went for the door. He pulled on it but it didn't open.

"Dude," the young man laughed and shook his head. "A deal's a deal."

"Deal? I make no deal. What is this?" Deon pulled on the door and it wouldn't move. "You make me trap? You make some kind of game?"

"Better yet. I want to fuck you." The young man jerked on his cock.

"You do not fuck me." Deon tugged the door once more and was about to bang on it.

"Bend over."

Deon watched the young man roll a condom on his cock and then use lubrication all the while filming it and him.

"Is this my nightmare?" Deon looked around the room for an escape. "What is going on? Why is this happening?"

"One way out, Frenchie." The creep pointed his cock at Deon.

Deon punched the door and shouted.

Another man entered, blocking Deon's way, wearing black leather and a cap. "Don't hit the door, dude or you're in for some serious hurt."

Deon spun around. "This is serious? You contain me and make demands?"

"I'm getting bored. Ya wanna take your pants down or have my buddy do it for you."

Deon looked from one man to the other. "You tape this? You know I will go to authorities. We do not call this consent!"

"Hey, dude. No one's gotta a gun to your head." The young man held up the camera.

Deon looked at the creep's henchmen and was not happy he had somehow been placed between a rock and a hard place. And not only that, David must be thinking he had either left or who knows what he could be doing to take so long.

Deon's hands shook and he muttered profanity as he faced the wall and took his pants to his thighs. "You pig! Filth!"

"Now, now, words like that will either make me horny or the porn video hotter than hell."

Deon felt hands on his hips and a cock near his ass. He looked to see the second man filming the contact. Deon hid his face turning the opposite way. "*La vengeance est un plat qui se mange froid mieux,* my friend," Deon said.

"Vengeance?" The young man moaned as he fucked Deon. "Yeah. You got that right, Deon. So right."

Deon heard the youth climax and pushed him off. He pulled his pants up and said, "You make deal."

"Let him out." The young man tugged the condom off.

Deon left the restroom and when he returned to the table, he found David standing, about to pay the tab. David stopped what he was doing and when he spotted Deon's expression he asked, "Where have you been?"

"I must go. Please."

Deon grabbed one of his security men and shoved him at Deon, "Get him to the car. Now."

The man held onto Deon. Deon hid his face from the crowded restaurant and was taken outside to a waiting sedan, complete with guarded escort. Before Deon entered the back of the sedan he said, "Where were you when I needed? Huh?"

"Senator Asher told us to back off. What the hell happened?"

"Nothing! Leave me!" Deon grabbed the inside of the door handle and slammed it, then grew furious and began punching at the interior of the car.

Chapter 3

David paid the tab and grabbed his head security man, walking out of the restaurant calmly as to not cause a scene. "What the heck happened?"

"I don't know, sir. You asked us to back off."

Outside by the car, David confronted his top security man. "Something happened in that men's room. I want you to get in there and find out what the hell it was. Look for witnesses, security cameras, I don't care! But find out."

"Yes, sir." The man returned to the restaurant.

David tried to control himself, inhaled to calm down, and then opened the back door of the car. He sat beside Deon who was in a heated state of anger.

David said nothing at first, allowing Deon his moment to decompress. When Deon did not speak, David said in a measured voice, "Are you going to tell me what just happened?"

Deon's fists clenched. "I no know what to do. What I can say."

"Did reporters get to you?" David was confused. "Did they ask you something?"

"Ask? No! I meet sick young man. Sick!"

"Sick." David interlaced his fingers. "You witnessed someone throwing up?"

"No." Deon shook his head. "I can no explain. Take me to hotel. I have no words now."

David leaned forward to the driver. "Get him back to his hotel."

"Yes, sir."

The car began to move.

David's phone hummed. He wanted to disregard it but glanced at it briefly. A photo of someone screwing Deon appeared on his phone.

"What the fuck?"

Then a caption came next from a blocked caller. *'think he liked being fucked? you're next.'*

"Deon!" David gaped at him. "Did someone harm you in the men's room?"

"What you see? No!" Deon reached for David's phone. He let out a whine and threw it back at David.

"Who is this?" David pointed to the phone.

"He...he same young man with champagne. He act like he work for hotel. I no know who is he. He kept me locked in."

"Oh, fuck this!" he said, "I'm calling the police."

The driver said quietly, "Speak to Eric Sutten first, sir."

"Fuck!" David dialed his chief of staff.

"David?"

"Where are you? I need a meeting. Now."

"In your office. Some new crap has hit the internet. I was about to call you."

"No." David shook his head and said loudly, "No!"

"Are you out with that model now, David?"

David could see Deon self-destructing. "Yes. He's a wreck."

"A wreck?"

"Wouldn't you be?" David didn't want to say anything that would further harm Deon's mental state.

"I'm reading a tweet. What are you talking about?" Eric's voice was calm.

David tried to take a deep breath as Deon slowly recuperated and began to appear less upset.

"What does the tweet say?" David did not want to know. He hated the social media and the capability it created of political homicide.

"It says hash-tag David Asher slut-fucker."

David felt physically ill. "Did…did any photo surface?"

"What type of photo am I looking for, David?" Eric sounded so serious David knew he was on edge.

"Not…not of me." David closed his eyes. "Was it from the same person who has been sending out these malicious messages?"

"No. It seems we have a clever little geek who understands how we track assholes. He keeps changing servers and we can't nail him down."

"Okay. Let me contact you later. I have other things to deal with at the moment." David disconnected the line and looked at Deon who was staring into space as the driver drove in the DC traffic.

"What do you want me to do?" David asked very softly.

Deon parted his lips as if he was going to answer then bit his bottom lip to stop the sentence.

"Do you want the police involved?" David yearned to touch Deon but after what he'd been through he had no idea if it was appropriate.

"No."

"So, this kid…" David tried to think. "Just some punk?"

"I no know why he target me? Hmm? Who am I to him?" Deon's fists clenched again. "I not have name here. I walk on fashion catwalk. No celebrity."

"Maybe you are not the target." David knew that sounded callous but it was what he was thinking.

"How not me?" Deon may have been burning lava of rage inside, but he controlled himself like a diplomat.

David felt the limousine stop and go in the traffic and grew frustrated he could not get Deon to his hotel where he most likely craved safety and a hot shower. "Ever since my staff and I have announced my candidacy for a White House run, I have become a target. We can't seem to pinpoint who it is, but it does seem as if we were followed to the restaurant…and…"

Deon met David's gaze.

"He somehow knew you and I were going to see each other. He found your hotel."

Deon looked out of the window. "He knows where I stay. Yes, he knows. I need different place."

David got back on his phone to his security staff.

"Yes, sir?"

"I need you to go to the Hyatt, room…" David looked at Deon.

"Twenty-thirteen."

"Twenty-thirteen," David repeated. "Clear it out, all the belongings. They belong to Deon Gael. He is being targeted by a crazy kid and needs to vacate."

"Yes, sir. To where?"

David cupped his phone. "To?"

"To?" Deon tilted his head.

"Where should your items be moved to?"

"Where is safe? Make new hotel?"

"Sir?" the security guard waited for direction.

There was a five star hotel a few blocks from where David's home was. David struggled with his own desires, the safety of Deon, and the desire to have this man closer to him.

He gave the high level security officer the instructions and the name of the hotel.

"Yes, sir."

David hung up and said to his driver, "Go to my home."

"Yes, sir."

"Is wise?" Deon asked.

"It's safe."

"No. Is no wise. Hotel."

David nodded reluctantly and told his driver, the name of the new hotel.

"I must tell my agent and assistant the change." Deon took out his phone and began dialing, speaking into the phone in French.

David began getting text messages from his staff, frantic ones about the new disparaging tweets.

He shut his phone. Leaning against the car door, he stared out of the tinted window, wondering who it could be. Who was his nemesis? A homophobic maniac? A technophobe off his meds?

Nothing had been easy for David, but he knew that from the start. He was never bullied. He fought. And even though someone had done something disgusting to Deon, David would not only find and prosecute the villain, he would triumph over him. And Deon did not deserve this humiliation, this violation.

Hearing his speaking in French, slightly heated but by far not the fury David would be spewing in his place, David respected Deon for his sensibility, the way he was handling a situation that so easily would have pushed a lesser man off the deep end.

When he felt Deon clench his thigh, David turned to him. As Deon spoke, more calmly, he held David, as if holding onto him for safety, for reassurance, for love. David reached for Deon, knowing now Deon did not want to be shunned by what happened, but wanted touch. Loving touch.

He embraced him, kissing his neck and holding him so tightly, the sense of yearning to kill his enemies needed to subside. The most powerful leader of the world had to keep a level head.

"*Oui…Merci. Nous parlerons demain…Oui…au revoir.*"

David heard Deon end the call, and then he pocketed the phone. When he did, Deon rested his head on David's shoulder, his hand gripped tightly to David's leg.

"You okay, Deon?"

"I will be. Yes. Just the surprise."

39

"What do you need me to do?" David held him close, pressing his lips against Deon's hair.

"Hold tight and make me forget."

David kissed Deon's hair and jaw.

Deon spun around and held David's cheeks and kissed him, whimpering and touching David's skin and hair.

David moaned against Deon's lips and kept squeezing his shoulders, digging his hand into his hair and then he embraced him, pressing his lips to Deon's ear. "I will be the one to avenge this. You do nothing but blank it out. You hear me?"

He felt Deon nod.

Then in his own ear David heard, "I am as you say, powerful. Not simple to topple. No act like this break my will."

"Then the two of us powerful men will manage to get rid of this pest. Do you understand?"

"Perfectly." Deon moved back so they could see eye to eye. "If what was done does not detest you in my eyes, I am still yours for pleasure."

Hearing the words of a warrior, not a victim, made David sexually wild. He cupped Deon's jaw and kissed him, open mouthed, and sucked at his tongue and lips.

Thinking he was by far the dominant male, David felt Deon making a move to get on top, nudging David so he was wedged into the corner by the door, and Deon had his hands against David's chest. The power shift had begun.

Not only did David feel it change in the kiss, he felt the strength of Deon's body. David served in war. He loved the fighting spirit, and nothing challenged him more mentally or physically than battle.

David parted from the kiss, breathless and slightly overwhelmed. Deon may appear like a pretty pet, but he was anything but.

Unable to help himself, David asked, through huffing breaths, "Why didn't you kick his ass?"

Deon narrowed his eyes at first in defensive fury. "The threat was to you, not me. This I know. Why would someone do such to a no name here? I see right through it."

David thought long and hard about that comment. "You allowed it to protect me?"

"I allow, thinking, if this what it takes, to stop from harm to you, then so be it." Deon backed away as the car seemed to stop, and engine shift to idle.

A door opened. Both men straightened their jackets and ties.

"Sir? The hotel?"

"One minute." David held up his finger.

The door was closed. David took a moment as Deon smoothed his hair and adjusted his collar and tie.

"You did that to protect me?"

Deon gave David a look of someone who has seen the ravages of war. "Sometimes one allows small victories to avoid big catastrophe. I would protect you. Yes."

David lunged for Deon, surprising him and making him jump, startled. David cupped Deon's face tenderly and did not mean to scare Deon by his abruptness. He whispered, "You are the most fantastic man I have ever met."

"You have not met all men." Deon smirked.

"No. But I have met one I will never forget. Or never stop wanting."

"I have heard comrades in arms do become close. Yes?"

"How do I get you in my bed?" David ran his hand down Deon's throat, over his tie.

"I wonder that as well." Deon looked at the hotel. "Where do you position your lover for you?"

David wanted to say, 'under me', but knew what Deon was asking. "Walking distance from my residence."

Deon smiled and tilted his head as if pondering the thought. "And who will walk?"

"Me."

"I see."

"My guard will escort you in. I assume it may take time to get your things from your hotel."

"You ask in cryptic way how long I need?"

"But I also respect what you have been through tonight, and if you need time to be on your own, you need only ask." David traced his finger over Deon's lips.

"This guard?" Deon gestured to the hotel. "He is now permanent fixture?"

"Damn right."

"Oh, so that will be news front page."

"Your safety is my top concern." David caressed Deon's hair. "He will be stationed outside your door, and accompany you when you are out."

"That is bodyguard. One from your staff?" Deon made a noise of disappointment. "This will not do. Our attacker wants this. You see? He wants you to be someone exposed. He is playing with your power."

"I don't mind the press knowing we are seeing one another."

"You mind when pictures of what happened make public, and suddenly you no lover with French model, you screwing *prostitué.* Say goodbye to your clean campaign. You see what he is up to. No good."

"I will ask again." David cupped Deon's jaw. "What do you want me to do?"

"Yes, I allow escort to room. For you. But I have staff. I will not use or…how you say, throw up in defeat hands. Nor do I need protection of man who is going to be next president. We allow attack to show how weak we are? No."

"But I want to catch this schmuck! I want to throttle him."

"And you no catch with armed guard." Deon wagged his finger at David. "And no win election with throttle."

"Then what?" David traced Deon's lips again, wanting to kiss him all night.

"I will have my own staff provide private security. Nothing to do with you, yes?"

"Okay."

"Perhaps..." Deon smiled, sucking one of David's fingers. "Later..." He swirled his tongue around it.

David moaned and his cock went thick.

"A handsome man will come to my door and..." Deon tapped the interior of the car. "Shhh. Tiptoe past the guard?"

David cupped Deon's jaw and kissed him, wildly, passionately. "You make me crazy."

"*Je vais être en attente*, I will be waiting." Deon smiled.

David released him and Deon exited the car. David climbed out of the backseat to watch his lover being escorted to the hotel.

The hot evening wind blew the dust around. The traffic was heavy, the scent of exhaust fumes filled his nose, and the sky was so full of artificial lights, David could barely see the stars.

He looked behind him, at one of his security guards in a car, watching him like a hawk. David leaned his arms on the top of his sedan and thought about this kind of life; one he had aspired to since he could remember. To be the President of the United States. When he was young he was laughed at for saying it out loud. As he worked his way through Harvard and to the top of his class, law review, big firms, powerful status, becoming a judge, then a mayor, then a senator, now...head on to becoming the democratic top pick for the next president. The first out gay man to hold that honor...

David began to wonder. That balance between power and personal life. It had been tenuous at best. Advisors everywhere, telling he and Lydia when to make their divorce public, keeping the family shielded, being honest, sharing his story with the press, his worries, his dreams, his hopes.

Seeing public humiliations occurring around him; politicians' dirty scandals, drug use, prostitutes making claims of sexual exploits, sexting- mayors and governors posting cock-shots online, taxpayer money being used for private parties and useless luxury not related to the office work...David had kept his nose clean. Or as clean as he could.

He remembered his father's words.

If you fuck up, fess up. Nothing they can do with the truth.

Even though he didn't have to prove a thing about his loyalty to the country, David enlisted in the army. Since he had such a high degree in law, he wasn't on the front lines, but he went there anyway. He was no office-computer warrior. He held a gun with the men on the ground.

How could he not? How could he judge their suffering, their pain if he did not see it himself? And since he had done it? He fought for their rights when others were trying to cut veteran's help and funding.

David swore if he ever had the chance to change things for the better he would. Slowly state by state, the loudmouth dinosaurs with skeletons in their closets were losing ground, while the youth and open-minded people's choices began to take hold.

He was told. Now was his time.

So David threw his hat into a ring. A fight he had a chance of actually winning. Until this.

Someone hated him. Hated him with so much venom, David was being crucified by this person. And he was trying so hard to think back, who? Who had he stepped on? In court, yes, he had to win battles. No one sent him threatening letters, nothing so over the top, he'd even reacted or reported anything.

As a mayor he may have made unpopular decisions, but was accountable. Attended town meetings, answered questions.

Nothing hit him like this.

But...David had never tried to gain this kind of political power.

And power brought out the worst in people.

Mostly from the ones wielding it, but…this was either jealousy or vengeance.

His security guard returned and said, "Mr Gael is safe in his room, sir."

"Did you clear that room?"

"I did, sir."

"Did Mr Gael register under his own name?"

"He used a credit card from his employer, and I suggested he not use his real name. The clerk behind the desk didn't question it when I showed my credentials. Shall I send someone to stand guard until Mr Gael has his belongings?"

"Mr Gael refused. He said he would hire private security through his own agency." David patted the man on the back. "But thank you."

"Sir." He was saluted and the guard moved towards the cavalcade of cars.

David looked at the line of black sedans and police escorts. In reality? With this type of parade you would think their cover would be blown. But in DC, escorts like this were everywhere.

Yet. If someone followed them from the fundraiser and to the restaurant? Did they then know when he and Deon left the restaurant? After Deon was assaulted?

David approached the young uniformed guard. "Can you stay anyway?"

"Sir?"

"Until Mr Gael's own security arrives."

"Yes, sir." The young man returned to the hotel.

David sat in his car and turned on his phone. It buzzed and vibrated with missed calls and messages. He put the phone to his ear as his driver took him to his residence.

"What?" he asked Eric, who had called a dozen times.

"The momentum has died down. I told everyone on our staff to disregard it. Let them think it's just some lunatic and not try to answer back or rebuff the insanity."

The car began to move.

"Has any videotape been uploaded? Any obscene photos show up?" David asked.

"None. Everyone is scanning the 'net, the blogs, your opponents' campaign ads, who, by the way, instead of jumping on this and disparaging you, aren't touching it."

"Well, it smells of a lunatic to me as well. Someone with a personal grudge. I certainly agree with my opponents not wanting to be a part of this smear campaign, But..."

"But?"

David could see they were pulling into to the front of his private home, which was surrounded by security gates and cameras.

"David, what are you not telling me? I'm your chief of staff. Tell me everything."

Before David got out of the car, he balled his fist. "I'm reluctant to."

"What on earth?" Eric sounded completely confused.

"I was out for dinner with Deon Gael, the French model."

"Yes. I know."

"He..." David tried to spit it out but was so angry he was growing out of control. "Someone trapped him in the men's room."

Eric said nothing.

"Trapped him and then blackmailed him."

"Blackmailed him."

David could tell Eric still could not understand. "In order to protect me, Deon had to do something against his will. And this freak..." David felt his body tense and his veins throb. "Videotaped it."

"What did he have to do? David!"

"The man fucked him!" David held the door closed when someone outside attempted to open it for him.

"Did you call the police? What did you do?"

46

"Deon refused it. Can you imagine the scandal?"

"And no one saw? No one witnessed anything?"

"There were two involved; one keeping people out of the men's room and recording it, and the one…"

"David. Calm down. I know you want to rip someone to shreds. I know you."

Eric!" David screamed, "I want revenge!"

"You show the world you are a man who cannot control his rage and how will it look? Huh? You'll be the crazy fucker who would nuke someone at the drop of a hat."

"Eric." David slouched in his seat, rubbing his face. "I like this man. He's kind. Intelligent."

"Breathe, David. Breathe. He's an adult. Okay? He can make decisions on how to deal with this without our input. If he wants us to make private inquiries we can. But keep it out of the public. You got it? Do not run to play the hero in this!"

"Eric, this idiot is targeting him to get at me. Don't play the hero? Don't help him?"

"I know you too well, David. You battle for the underdog constantly. You hate when right is wronged. I know you. But if you let this get under your skin, this fucker will ruin you, ruining your chances to get into the White House with it. So calm the fuck down!"

David tried to take a few deep breaths.

"Where are you?" Eric asked.

"Home. Parked out front. I just had him relocated because this fucking lunatic knows where he is staying at the hotel."

"You relocated him? You did?"

"Eric," David said in warning.

"You could call me, call Leona, call Terry, you have a staff David! For fuck's sake!"

"He's mine! I mean." David rubbed his face. "He's my responsibility."

"Jesus, please don't tell me you have fallen for a young French runway model."

"Shut up!" David growled.

"David. Calm down and listen to me."

"I'm about to fire you and hang up."

"David."

He was breathing fire but listening.

"How long have you known me?" Eric asked.

"All my fucking life." David rubbed his eyes since they felt gritty and dry.

"David, I knew your dad. I knew you when you were in a bassinette."

David listened quietly.

"You have to trust me."

"I do." David looked around the car. His men were motionless waiting for him.

"Do not let your fucking political career go down the toilet for a fashion model."

"No, Eric, he's more than that."

"David."

Eric's tone shut David up.

"I was there at the fundraiser. I know who Deon Gael is. He's a twenty-nine year old bombshell. Okay? He's perfection. For an affair."

"Careful, Eric." David grew livid.

"It's like these straight candidates who love the arm candy. David…he's gone toxic with this new lunatic attached to him. Let. Him. Go."

David made a noise of grief in his throat.

"Are you hearing me or just humoring me, David?"

David didn't know what to say.

"You want to be the next president? Huh? Or stick with the senate? That is, *if* you're lucky after the damage some deranged geek will do to you."

"So? Just abandon Deon? When we have the resources to—"

"David."

David began to get a headache.

"You cannot use your political resources to find this moron. If the moron was targeting you or your family, yes, but not a pretty French model. I asked you a question. Are you hearing me or humoring an old man?"

David exhaled in complete frustration.

"Now, get in your home, drink some sherry, and stop. You will meet many men. Fabulous men. You are out, you are divorced, there is no scandal attached to you. Do not, I repeat, do not see this man again."

David stared at the phone.

"David?"

He disconnected it and got out of the car.

His personal bodyguard walked silently with him to the front door, where he was posted. And the line of escorts and sedans vanished from his sight.

David thanked the man as he opened the door for him.

"Goodnight, sir."

"Goodnight." David stood for a moment in the entranceway of the home, hearing the dead silence of the empty rooms.

He loosened his tie and made his way to the kitchen. As he did, he turned on lights. His phone continued to hum, so he glanced at it. His press secretary, Leona, his staff assistant, Terry…even the legislative director, and correspondents had texted him. Some said, '*it will blow over, sleep well,*' while others said, '*everyone is ignoring the jerk, don't worry*'.

He set the phone down on the counter, and took off his suit jacket and tie, then unbuttoned the collar of his shirt. He poured a glass of sherry as Eric suggested and sipped it, standing in the empty room.

His phone hummed.

Weary of it, wishing he could just relax, he glanced down and saw who it was from. He grabbed it.

"*Bonsoir, mon amour.*"

Just the sound of Deon's voice made David weak at the knees. "Did…Are you safe?"

"Yes. Safe, but lonely. Very lonely."

The warnings of his chief of staff, like orders from a commander, echoed in David's head. He knew ignoring it for a sexual fling was a very bad idea. "I…I thought after your ordeal you may want to just rest."

"Yes. I too, thought that. So I took a hot bath, washed the body, but the mind, does not cleanse so easily."

"I'm sorry. Again, what can I do? Do you want me to see if I can—"

"Hush, lover, you try so hard to please, and please. You give to everyone. Who, hmm? Who gives to you?"

David finished the sherry and set the glass aside. "I don't need much. I'm a busy man."

"*Oui*, busy with paper, with meetings, with commands to change good from bad. But what about David Asher the man? Hmm?"

David rubbed his face and sighed. "He's okay."

"This former wife, she was good wife?"

"Yes. And she's a good friend to me now as an ex-wife. I'm lucky."

"She give you what you need now? A way to release?"

David tried to think about what Deon implied. "Not sexually, is that what you mean?"

"No, David, no, I mean the head. Mentally. She let you steam outside your mind?"

David smiled at the way Deon said his name, '*Dah-vid*' and his explanations were priceless. "Not really. Lydia is a very busy woman, involved in many charities and women's groups."

"Then who takes care of the man? Hmm? The man, not the politician?"

"I'm fine."

"You tell me fine. I believe. I don't become the crazy with the champagne and camera."

David's smile faded. "No, I don't mean that. I don't want you to ever think I imagine you that way."

"But now? Huh? With this menace. Our simple meetings are not so simple. He has, how you say…"

David made his way to his sofa in the darkness of the living room and sank into it. "Yes. He has, as we say, ruined it."

"So, *fini*? That is the saga of the politician and the French model?"

"Oh, God…" David craved him and rubbed his hand between his legs over his cock.

"I understand. We have nice night, yes? Beautiful dinner. Some sweet kisses. Is good. I have little chapter in your book, maybe?"

"How…" David cleared his throat. "How long will you be in town?"

"Week, I think? I have several shows I must participate. Here and nearby here. I could check my calendar. Are you interested?"

Knowing he should say no, David said, "Yes."

"So public? At large gatherings of designers? Is good idea?"

"I may be able to see you again after. After you strut the catwalk like a lion."

When Deon laughed it made David smile.

"A lion. Yes. I am no pussy cat. You know this."

David found his personal planner on his phone. He scanned the week ahead. "Can you email me your itinerary?"

"Of course, Senator. For you, I can do anything."

David closed his eyes in agony. "I want you here. You have no idea."

51

"Sex? For the sex?"

David sank deeper into the sofa's soft cushions. "I am sexually attracted to you, I won't lie."

"Phew!" Deon chuckled. "I was hoping the incident did not taint me...you know."

"No! No..." David tried to calm down. "But I sense more to you. I just know you must leave DC and I feel as if I will never get to know Deon Gael the man, not just the fabulous model."

"Oh, you say just the right things, *mon amour*. Coming from a man such as yourself. It brings me to chills."

David leaned his elbows on his knees. "What are you wearing?"

He heard a low chuckle.

"Tell me." David smiled.

"A white towel."

"And?"

"And?

"Nothing more?" David began to pace, feeling like a caged prisoner.

"A hot bath, a sip of cognac, and you. That is what so far has happened. Oh, and my items arrive in good order, and my assistant has hired a private watchdog. He is near, I believe. Outside my room."

David's heart sank. "Then if you were to come here, or I am to go there..."

"Can be seen. But we ask for this. Both, to stop the maniacs. What to do?"

David stopped pacing. "What is he wearing?"

"Who wearing what this time?"

"The guy, the guard."

"Oh, let me peek."

David looked outside his own private residence, one where he lived full time for the last two years; since he was officially divorced.

It wasn't as if his commute was long. He was the state senator of Maryland and his ex-wife still lived in the house they owned together.

Hired off-duty DC police officers kept guard over him during high profile events. But when it came to his own security, he bought his own private guards. With the terrorists and the homegrown nutters, most high ranking government personnel had some kind of protection. And ever since David became a strong viable presidential candidate, Eric insisted the guards be permanent and sadly, ubiquitous.

"Dark blue, shirt and pants. Some kind of badge, no police words, other something. Possibly say security company name? But he carries police-like-armed belt with gun."

"You went out with just your towel on?"

"You ask to look! I just peek. He see me and ask if I am okay, I say yes."

"Deon."

"David."

"You are not just a sexual object for me."

"Not just. What am I to hear from you?"

"I mean…look. Do you want me there?"

"Here? Is it possible? With everything—"

"Deon," David interrupted him. "Do you want me there?"

"Yes."

"Then I will go."

"But do not do this to risk—"

"Deon, my lion?"

"Yes?" Deon laughed.

"I am on my way."

"Your lion awaits."

David hung up, hustled to the front of his residence and waved one of the men towards him. The man rushed over. "Sir?"

"Get in here." He took a look at the man's height and weight.

"Is there something wrong?"

"Take off your uniform." David kicked off his own shoes and unbuttoned his shirt.

"Huh?"

"That's an order." David knew the man was stunned but placed his brimmed dark hat on the coffee table in the dim living room and set his gun belt down. David piled his pants and shirt on the sofa and began getting dressed in the young man's uniform.

"Am I going to go to jail for this…sir?"

"No. Put my clothing on. Sit on the sofa." David dressed in the man's uniform and put the gun belt on, then checked the guard's wallet and tossed it at the man after taking the guard's ID. David headed to the kitchen and returned with a bottle of beer. He turned on the television, handed the young man getting dressed in his clothing the remote control and said, "Raid the fridge. There's a ton of food. Don't answer the phone. Got it?"

"Are you kidding me?" The young man buttoned the shirt, then took the remote.

"No. And you are under strict orders to keep your trap shut. Am I understood?" David cracked open a beer and put it on a coaster on the low coffee table. "Oh, I have premium cable, just avoid the gay channels. Some of them are porn."

"How…how long will you be gone, sir?" The young man looked nervous.

"How long are you supposed to be outside my premise until you are relieved?"

"Until zero-two-hundred hours, sir."

David winked, put a pair of dark aviator sunglasses on, gave him a thumbs-up and left the house.

POWER PLAY

Chapter 4

Deon made sure he was properly cleaned, inside and out, groomed to perfection and left the bathroom to turn down the bed. He wore a white terrycloth bathrobe, one supplied by the hotel, which was five star and had all the amenities one would desire, including a full bar.

He stood near the balcony and stared out at the city, the lights of the nation's capital, glittering as the summer sun finally grew weary and began to sink.

In the distance Deon could see the Washington Monument, and other iconic attractions, becoming spotlighted. He had been to the US so many times, to all the big cities, he did not need to tour it for his leisure. Most of the trips were to Los Angeles or New York.

But he went where they needed him. A fundraiser this time. He was always happy to help. And when he found the campaign and cause he was assisting, Deon became smitten by the man behind the scenes. One who battled for the poor and needy.

But, it was a silly crush. Two men, opposite worlds. Just a fun romp.

How would David come here without scrutiny?

Deon made sure two glasses were set out and inspected the choice of beverages.

As he waited he flipped through a menu for room service, but other than perhaps fruit or cheese, later, he was still full from dinner.

His phone hummed and thinking of David, Deon rushed to see it. It was from Clair. A text message telling him what time he would be picked up in the morning and to eat before he left the hotel because there would be very little to eat at the next event.

Deon acknowledged her and set the phone down, growing bored. He sat on the foot of the bed and turned on the television. Each channel left him uninterested and restless. Just as he shut it off, he heard a conversation outside his door. Deon jumped to his feet and rushed to look out of the peephole.

The private security guard was talking to another man in uniform. Deon grew concerned and immediately opened the door.

"What is the problem?" Deon asked.

A man in uniform, his cap pulled low on his forehead, wearing dark glasses showed an ID quickly and said, "From the US Secret Service." He didn't even wait to see the reaction of the private security guard, who was speechless. And of course secret service agents did not wear private security guard outfits. But this man didn't stop to think as David loomed powerful and threatening.

Deon instantly recognized David and covered his laughter.

David nudged Deon into the room and told the other security guard, "Just a few questions for Mr Gael and I'll be done."

"Yes, sir." The guard nodded and appeared impressed.

Deon held in his laughter as he was brought to the bedroom. Once he was far enough away from the door he looked at David and shook his head in amazement. "You do not do this. I am struck silent."

David grinned. "Ya like it?" He held out his arms.

"I like of course, because it is you. I no have police uh…"

"Fetish?"

"Fetish?" Deon tilted his head since he had never heard the word.

"Forget it." David grabbed Deon and picked him up, toss him on the bed. He flung his cap and sunglasses aside and went for Deon's mouth.

Deon moaned as his robe was parted and this man, who was already a powerhouse in a suit and tie was now in uniform with a loaded gun. Maybe Deon was attracted to this. It was certainly exciting him.

David leaned up to look at Deon. "Oh, holy Christ."

Deon peeked down at his naked body, then at David. "Is all you want a quick look?"

David licked his lips and ran his hand from Deon's jaw to his low abdomen. "I don't think I have ever been with a man as perfect as you."

"No such thing as perfection." Deon waved him off. "Attain at peril. We are but creatures, and some take care, some do not."

"Uh, buddy. You won the genetic lottery." David started to laugh.

Deon had no idea what he meant but began unbuttoning the uniform shirt. "Who is 'Smith' and is he now naked?"

David stripped off the uniform shirt and stood, taking off his lower half of clothing as he stared at Deon's body. "He's one of my private security staff, and no. He is comfy on my sofa drinking beer and watching cable TV."

Deon laughed and shook his head. "You either smart or very, very in trouble."

Once David was naked he dove on top of Deon and began nibbling his neck. "I'm hoping to be smart. And happily sated."

"Mm. I hope this mean good thing." Deon reached down and stroked David's cock. "You are big man."

"Grrr." David chewed on Deon's neck trying to get him to spread his legs with his knees.

"So eager to get in. How you know I no want in you."

"You can. I just have to prepare for you." David licked his way to Deon's mouth.

Deon opened his lips and held David's cock in his hand. The feel and scent of this man was making him swoon. He pushed David to his back and parted from the kiss. "You want lion or lamb?" Deon began kissing his way down David's chest.

"Oh fuck!" David ran his hand over his hair and propped his head up so he could watch. "What a choice!"

"Hmm?" Deon sucked David's cock, just putting the head in his mouth teasingly.

"You gorgeous, motherfucker!" David reached down for Deon but did not pull him or push him to make a decision.

~

You are the type of man to take down a career. My fucking God. Look at you. David was so excited he was going to embarrass himself and come the minute this man did anything more to him. The body on Deon was like Michelangelo's David. Not perfect? Where was this man's imperfection?

Deon released David's cock from his mouth and ran his hand over the hair on David's chest. "So nice you no need wax, shave. You are man. I like."

"Oh, babe, I have no need to preen. On the contrary. But I do think keeping fit is essential."

"So fit." Deon ran his hand over David's chest.

"I want to fuck you." David hoped it was okay since the incident at the restaurant. "But I understand it if—"

Deon, as if he knew what was coming, held up his hand and silenced David. "The lamb you shall have." He narrowed his eyes wickedly. "Tonight."

David grabbed Deon and rolled them both over, so Deon was under him.

"But next time, you shall have the lion." Deon touched the tip of David's nose and smirked.

David drew that finger into his mouth and sucked it. Deon gave him the most eloquent whimper of sexual longing he had ever heard.

He gripped Deon's cock and sucked his finger at the same time. As he swirled his tongue around Deon's finger, showing him what he wanted to do to his dick, he squeezed and jerked Deon's perfect straight cock.

Deon began to moan and writhe on the bed under him, gripped to David tightly and spreading his legs.

David released his suction on Deon's finger and went for his lips.

Deon arched his back and came, gasping against David's mouth.

David parted from the kiss to see it, see the cum splashing Deon's skin. "Oh fuck! Where the hell is a rubber?"

"There." Deon pointed. "In drawer." He closed his eyes and rocked his hips side to side.

David lunged for the nightstand and tore a condom open with his teeth, rolling it on, then using the lubrication that was with it. He knelt on the bed and jerked his own cock, riding the edge as he stared at this French god and the creamy spatter on his tanned skin.

"I'm about to blow. Holy fuck."

"In. In." Deon spread his legs and beckoned David.

It had been so long since he had made love to a man, David knew he wasn't going to last, and maybe, because of what Deon had endured, that wasn't a bad thing. He pushed in gently and Deon made the penetration deep and fast.

David felt a rush so strong he closed his eyes and gripped Deon's knees. There was no holding back. He was over the cliff and falling.

David thrust in fast and hard a few times and choked on his climax, closing his eyes, bracing himself on the bed and shivering from the intensity. He literally could not move for a few seconds and was floored by the pleasure. He pulled out and shook his head. "I'm sorry. It's been so damn long."

"Sorry?" Deon tilted his head and touched the sticky drops on his skin. "The lion apologizing to the lamb?" Deon laughed.

David tugged off the condom and dropped it on the floor, then lay down on top of Deon. "You think you're a funny guy."

"I no think I ever going to hear Mr President-to-be swear like a street boy."

David felt his cheeks blush and avoided his gaze. "Sorry. I suppose it was undignified."

"It was hot!" Deon growled and snapped his jaws playfully.

David cupped Deon's cheek tenderly and stared at him. "I don't want to, but I have to go."

"Yes. I know."

Rolling off Deon to lay beside him, David ran his hand through the stickiness left on Deon's skin. He tasted it from his finger and Deon made a noise of pure pleasure as he witnessed it.

Feeling Deon's tender touch, David met his fabulous baby blue eyes.

"I never would think of you as such a man."

David could see Deon's affection for him and it was going to make leaving him tonight that much harder.

"Not so much for the touch, but the manner. Do I make sense?" Deon caressed David's cheek.

David kissed his hand. "I don't know if it made sense, but with your accent, anything sounds amazing."

Deon laughed and pushed him playfully. "You the one with accent."

David stood, looking down at Deon then the pile of clothing on the floor. He picked up the used condom and headed to the bathroom to toss it out. He stared at himself in the mirror.

His smile faded.

One would think the man that may be the next most powerful leader of the free world would be free to do as he liked.

He looked down at his skin, which glistened from Deon's cum. If he was in his own clothing, he would not wash, he would keep it on him to linger as he slept.

But…

David grabbed a washcloth and saved the security guard the pleasure of spunk aroma on his gear.

Deon stepped in, lightly, like a dancer, and slipped his arms around David from behind, seeing both their reflections in the mirror.

David finished washing up and leaned against Deon.

"We make handsome couple. No?"

David looked at them together. "Yes. We do."

"I see you again?" Deon rocked him, kissing David's shoulder.

David closed his eyes as the warning of his chief of staff and the possibility that he had already been caught missing from his home began to invade his thoughts.

As if Deon could read his expression like spoken words, Deon released David and stepped back. "I know you do what you can. I know."

David met his gaze and opened his hands in a gesture of pure helplessness. "It's not because I don't want you."

Deon bit his bottom lip and looked away. "Of course. Yes."

David approached him. "Look for a message from me tomorrow."

"Good. Yes."

He used a towel to wipe his back in case the embrace left a trace of cum on him.

David could tell Deon was hurt, but what could he do? He returned to the bedroom and put the security guard's clothing back on. Deon, naked, watched him, leaning on the bathroom doorway.

David put on the gun-belt, picked up the cap and sunglasses and made sure he had everything he had come with. He placed the cap on his head and looked at Deon. "I will get my lion."

Deon braved a smile. "Yes, of course."

"Do I get a kiss goodbye?"

Deon rushed him and went for David's lips. David held him tight, rocking him, not wanting to let him go.

Slowly they stopped kissing, holding each other, foreheads pressed together. David stepped back. He put the sunglasses on and tugged the cap low. "Do I look like me?"

Deon smiled. "You will always look like you...to me."

David threw him a kiss and walked to the door. He glanced back once, took in Deon's fabulous naked body, and then opened the door. The security man nearly stumbled at the surprise. David said, as he closed the door behind him. "Good job. Make sure no one gets in."

"Yes, sir."

David jogged down the steps and out into the DC night. He didn't rush, he walked, through the grass, bypassing lit up streets, and headed to his home. He spotted a black sedan parked out front and swore under his breath. He began to hurry, holding the gun to his hip and entered the home.

The young man he left behind was being interrogated by Eric Sutten. The moment David showed up, Eric spun around and appeared stunned.

David tossed off the cap and sunglasses. "Don't even think of blaming that kid." He began taking off his uniform shirt.

The young man took off David's shirt and slacks. "I didn't say a thing, sir. I didn't know where you went."

"Smith." David tossed him his clothing. "Stop worrying. Get dressed and go home."

"Yes, sir." The young man put his clothing on quickly, and once he had his cap on his head, he said meekly, "My ID, Senator?"

Standing in his briefs, David dug through his wallet and gave the young man the ID then waited for him to leave. The look on Eric's face was of pure disbelief.

David held up his hand. "Do not even say it." David put his slacks on and then headed to the kitchen.

"Are you out of your mind?" Eric pursued him.

David opened a decanter of bourbon and poured a shot, tossing it back and swallowing it.

"You are this close!" Eric made a gap in his fingers to show the tiny space. "And you are masquerading as a security guard to go screw that model?"

"Eric?" David held up his finger. "Not now. Not tonight."

"You have the fucking support of the party. You have enough donor cash to back you right through to the campaign. What are you doing? You have never led your actions with your penis! Never!"

David poured another shot and downed it. He couldn't look at Eric. Wouldn't.

"Don't become one of those casualties. David, you are so close. Don't end up a laughing stock like the others. The fools who screwed up their political careers only to be mocked and ridiculed by the opposition on radio shows and horrid news channels."

David set the empty glass aside and placed both his palms on the counter. He stared through the glass doors of his cabinet to the plates neatly stacked inside. "I feel as if I am a prisoner."

"You can socialize with men, David."

David didn't want 'men'.

"Why this one? Why? Is he that beautiful that he has you under his spell? So much so you will risk everything you have aspired to all your life?"

"Eric. Stop." David closed his eyes. He wished he could smell Deon on his skin. He tried to sniff his shoulder but could sense nothing.

Eric's voice grew calmer, and David could feel him move closer, standing behind him. "David."

David would not turn around to look at Eric. It would be like facing his own father, and to have disappointed his late-father this way…well, it was unthinkable.

"David. Let him go. Please. The terrible scandal associated with this model, it is not going away."

At that comment, David spun around, fury sparking. "What happened?"

"The tweets! Those miserable comments about you being seen with a prostitute. David, use sense."

Relief washed over him. "Oh. I thought…"

"David." Eric touched David's shoulder lightly. "You're a great man. A man this country is starving for. You could do so much for so many. Your record is spotless. You are loved. Loved. Truly."

"Loved." David shook his head. "By strangers. By people who push voting buttons."

"Yes. Isn't that the whole meaning of this? To gain the respect and admiration of the world? To shine? To show just what kind of man you can be to lead us into the next four years?"

David finally met Eric's eyes. They were the same color as his father's. A light bluish gray. And Eric reminded David of his dad so much. "I'm sorry."

"David." Eric shook his head gently, admonishing.

"I get lonely. You know Lydia and I…" David didn't have to tell Eric the history. Eric was there through it. "I don't date. I don't go out with…" He gestured around the kitchen. "Men." David wiped at his nose roughly. "Even though I am out I think people would be turned off. I mean, yeah, they know I'm gay, but do they want to see me holding a man's hand? Huh? Kissing one?"

Eric said nothing, listening.

"Sure, I can go out to dinner. Be social." David shrugged. "I'm not afraid to be 'seen'," he used air quotes, "with a man, in a man's company. But…to find someone I truly like. Want to make love to?"

Eric looked away, as if he didn't want to hear it.

David read it instantly. "You see? I am to be a celibate gay president."

Eric began to walk to the living room. "I am not telling you to be celibate." He picked up his walking stick, then stopped to speak to David. "I am saying, choose wisely."

David approached him, standing near the threshold of the front door. "And what if the next man I decide to be social with gets nailed like this one did. And the next."

Eric tilted his head. "You think that's what's happening? No matter which man you see on a social level that this will be the case?"

David shrugged. "I don't know. I've been so busy I can't recall the last man I have went out on a date with."

"We have to find this punk." Eric walked to the front door. "I hope we do." Eric looked back at David before he opened the door. "Or, my good friend, you will be a very lonely man."

David clenched his jaw in frustration.

"Goodnight, David."

"Goodnight, Eric." David watched as a guard walked his chief of staff to the waiting car. Before shutting the door, he spotted a different security guard posted out front. David closed and locked the door, then stood still in the silence.

He repeated softly. "A very lonely man."

Chapter 5

Saturday morning, David sipped a cup of coffee, watching the news and reading the morning paper. He heard someone at his front door and stood from his breakfast nook to see who it was. When he realized it was his daughter, Veronica, he opened his arms in greeting.

His coffee cup high in the air, his twenty-one year old daughter gave him a hug. Wearing a T-shirt, shorts and sandals, she opened his cupboard and poured herself a cup of coffee.

"To what do I owe this honor?" He smiled and watched her tip milk into a mug and was always happy when his kids stopped by.

"Bored. Summer break is too long." She tossed her straight blonde hair over her shoulder and leaned her elbows on the island counter to look at the newspaper her father was reading.

"Have you had breakfast?" He set his cup down. "I can make you something."

"Yeah. I ate yoghurt at Mom's." She looked up from the paper. "I really wanted to see how you are."

David's smile fell slightly. "How should I be?"

"Come on, Dad." She set the cup down and turned a page of the newspaper. "I don't live under a rock."

He sat on a stool across from her at the island counter and held his coffee mug. "I'm okay."

She pouted and met his eyes. "I think it's really shitty. Fucking nerds."

"Speaking of nerds...have you heard from your brother at all?"

She shrugged. "He hangs with his geek friends in some garage. Jim thinks he's going to be the next Mark Zuckerberg or Steve Jobs." She picked up an apple from a bowl of fruit on the counter and bit it. As she chewed she said, "But he's just a dweeb."

David thought about his nineteen year old son. "He used to stop by more. I was thinking. Do you want to go on a family vacation when the senate session ends on July Fourth?"

She rolled her eyes at him. "I'm twenty-one, not ten."

"Oooh, sorry!" He laughed at her and sipped his coffee.

She turned another page of the newspaper. "So, tell me about this French guy."

David looked at the paper but wasn't really seeing it, since not only was it upside down, he became lost in his thoughts. He didn't know why, but he was surprised she knew about Deon. He wasn't big on the tabloid press and his staff only kept him up to date on damage control or bad information, not a snapshot of him having dinner with a friend.

"Dad?"

"Huh?" David gave her his attention.

"He's really handsome. I looked him up on the 'net. Are you going to date him?"

"I...with...with the tweets..." David stuttered, not knowing what to say.

"Oh, pah-leeze!" Veronica rolled her eyes. "You think I would stop seeing a hottie because of some basement loser who probably picks his nose and is a virgin at thirty?"

He laughed and set his mug down. "You, young lady, are not running for president."

"And you shouldn't let a freak who has too much time on his hands decide who you can date." She took another bite from the apple, then tossed it out. As she chewed she stood beside him and leaned on his shoulder. "Mom told me you don't go out on dates at all."

"Mom needs to keep those thoughts to herself."

"Dad. I don't mean to sound like a weirdo or anything, but…" She sighed loudly. "You're still handsome. You can go out with guys. You came out! Why did you divorce mom and come out to the public and then go all shy and not see any men?"

"I divorced your mother because it was the right thing to do for both of us." He gently pushed her long hair behind her shoulder with one finger. "I came out because I am not only proud to be gay, I am honest."

She leaned her head on his shoulder and let out a loud breath of what sounded to David as frustration.

"And I don't really date, because I think the difference between people knowing I like men…and seeing me…with a man, will make some people wince in the polls."

"They need to grow up." She stood back and checked her phone.

"When was the last time you spoke to Jimmy?" David watched her use her thumbs to text quickly, her nails were painted blue.

"Umm." She finished her text and appeared to think harder. "He asked me if I knew of someone who had a legal weed permit."

David was not pleased. "When?"

She scrolled through her messages. "About a week ago? I told him no, and he needed to keep me out of his drug shit."

"He is still planning on going back to college this September, right?"

"Ya know, Dad?" Veronica put her phone in her purse. "Jim and I don't talk much anymore. I mean, we have nothing in common. And…I don't like him."

David was about to make a comment about how wrong that was, but she added, "He's hanging with some weird guys. I don't know. Ask Mom. I don't deal with his stuff." She pecked her father on the cheek and said, "Date the hunk, will ya?"

David stood off the stool and walked her to the front door. "Do you at least want to go out to dinner or something soon?"

She shrugged. "Sure. Just text me." She pecked his cheek again. "Bye."

He stood at the door as she walked to the curb where she parked her little Mini. A guard stood near his door, but they didn't interact. David watched Veronica drive off and she beeped as if saying goodbye.

David closed the door and checked his watch, then finished getting ready for a quick Saturday morning meeting with his staff before the next working day of senate debates and hearings on Monday.

~

At a private salon; one which Clair had arranged to be used exclusively for Gabriel, their own stylist, and their stable of models, Deon sat in a chair in front of a mirror. At the moment, he was the only model being tended. A plastic apron was snapped around his neck and Gabriel was standing behind him with scissors. Clair was on the phone, speaking French to someone about the next event, as Gabriel touched the ends of Deon's dark hair.

"Long," Gabriel said.

Clair cupped the phone, "Shorter!"

"He looks good with long hair!" Gabriel ran his fingers through Deon's thick dark locks. "What do you want him to look like? A convict from prison?"

Deon sighed and grew impatient.

"Shorter!" Clair went back to her phone call, giving the men her back.

Gabriel bent down to Deon's ear and said, "She is a bitch. I'm just trimming it."

Deon waved at him dismissively, thinking of David, wondering if he worked weekends.

Gabriel began combing and snipping just the ends of his hair.

He heard Clair use a loud French expletive, and then she turned to look at Deon.

"What?" he asked her in French at her outraged expression.

She whispered into the phone and then disconnected it and appeared pained.

Gabriel kept trimming. "I'm not cutting it short."

"Clair. What is it?" Deon folded his hands on his lap under the apron.

"A photo has surfaced of you."

"What photo?" Deon asked.

Gabriel echoed it, also speaking French.

More muttered swear words came from Clair and she held her smart-phone in her hand so tightly her knuckles were turning white.

"What?" Deon yelled at her in annoyance.

She held out the phone. A picture from an instant photo application showed him naked coming out of the shower in the hotel he had stayed at previous to moving.

Deon sat up and pushed the apron aside to study it. "How was this taken?"

"Who was in the shower with you?" Gabriel looked.

Deon hid it against his chest so Gabriel could not see it and stared at Clair. "No one! No one was in the shower with me!"

Gabriel put his hands on Deon's shoulder. "Someone planted a camera in that bathroom. Talk about a violation of your privacy! I would call and complain right now."

Clair grabbed the phone, pushing buttons and Deon could hear her yelling at someone from the last hotel's management.

Deon rubbed his forehead in misery. "Why? Hmm? Why are they doing this to me? To ruin me? To ruin my career, my life?"

Gabriel stopped cutting Deon's hair. "Sue the bastards. That's just sick."

Deon tried to sit straight in the chair so Gabriel could finish. As he did, he began to think of David and grew upset. "No. Stop. I can't sit here anymore." Deon stood up from the chair and tugged off the apron.

Gabriel looked helpless and Clair was screaming into the phone in broken English.

Deon brushed his hand over his hair and straightened his cotton short-sleeved shirt. "Tell Clair I must leave. To clear my head. I am going out of my mind."

Gabriel nodded and stood still.

Deon left the salon and looked up at the bright sun. He put his sunglasses on and began walking down the street. As he did he text David. *'He has posted me nude in shower now.'*

Deon did not know David's schedule but did crave to see him. He heard a footstep close behind him and stopped and turned around in paranoia. A busy shopper was passing by, her phone to her ear, bags in her free hand, and nearly ran him over.

Since the incident in the restaurant, Clair had arranged for private security for Deon. Now he was torn between going back to the salon and having her call someone to watch over him. But needing a bodyguard gave him the sense of claustrophobia and made him wonder if he was indeed paranoid.

His phone rang. He saw it was Clair. He knew she was furious he had left. Ignoring it, he kept walking, ending up where tourists flooded the large landscaped park of the National Mall. Out in the distance was the Lincoln Memorial.

Tour buses crept slowly by as the heat and humidity began to gain momentum with the passing morning. Deon kept his eye on the massive columned structure at the end of the park as he walked, without purpose or reason, towards it.

G. A. HAUSER

He glanced at the water of the reflecting pool and knew it was a much longer walk to the building than it seemed. And in the humid heat, it was making him drip with sweat.

He dabbed at a drop running down his temple and continued with the other pedestrians; some with maps, others wearing brimmed caps to keep the sun off their faces.

After a long walk, Deon stood looking up at the impressive building. He had never been inside.

As he drew near the front steps, tour groups to each side of him, Deon continued to make his way upwards. The numerous steps became irrelevant as he caught sight of the enormous seated statue of Abraham Lincoln. Deon stopped, midway- one foot up, the other on the stair behind him, and looked at the enormous sculpture, admiring the craftsmanship. He was so used to Europe, spoiled on the history, the magnificence of their own artists and architects, he had to admit, like many of his European neighbors, not much in the U.S. compared to their art and architecture, built on centuries of history. While here, in this young country, born only in 1776, old was something from the 50s.

Where he was from? *Old* was thousands of years ago.

He looked back, behind himself, at the area as a whole. The pool was shimmering and trees lined both sides, very picturesque.

After seeing some of the landmarks of the nation's capital, he smiled to himself. Yes. There was some impressive architecture here. *History for this 'toddler' of a country*. Was he a snob? Perhaps.

His phone hummed and if it was a text from Clair he was going to scream. Yes, he had an event this evening, yes, he knew when he had to be there …yes, yes…

Then he read it was from David. All it said was, '*where are you?*'

Deon held the phone to his heart and turned once again to see the icon of what, the world, not only The United States, considered to be one of the greatest historical figures of all time.

He typed back, '*may I call?*'

His phone rang. Deon put it to his ear. "David?"

"I just read the text. What nude photo? Where is it posted?"

"I not know site. Clair show me. Now. Just before." Deon looked back towards the direction he had come. "I look as if camera was inside the shower of old hotel I stay. How can this be? They do this here? This invasion?"

"What? Are you kidding me?"

"Why I kid about this? No. She showed me picture. I can see it myself."

"No, I didn't mean..." He heard David exhale loudly. "Are you okay?"

"Yes." Deon walked near the shade of the trees, feeling the sun's heat. "I, myself, am fine. What I can do? I have to let go. Clair call hotel and she will make trouble. But I have no desire." He moved nearer a large tree for the deeper shade. "I ask same thing. How are you?"

"About to call the hotel myself at the moment."

"No. Let Clair. She can be very...how you say? Fight-full."

"Still, I think it may be the freak who is stalking you, not the hotel. But she can at least inquire."

"Yes. I suspect this too. Why would hotel risk such reputation?"

David asked, "What is your schedule like today?"

Deon smiled. "I wonder same of you. I ask myself is he work Saturday?"

"I had a quick meeting with my staff this morning, but I don't have to be back on the job until Monday."

"Does this mean free time?" Deon smiled and looked at the buses with tourists pointing their cameras at the monuments.

"I can always tell my minders I'm at the gym."

Deon laughed and began walking back from the direction he had come. "I too, have minders. We both have leash. Yes?"

"Sadly. Crazy huh? You'd think two men with our status and power would be free to do as we wish."

"No. No, David, not when public eye is on. No." Deon looked up at the busy streets.

"Where are you?"

"I just take walk. Clear head."

"Are you with a bodyguard?"

"No. No need. I had trim of hair and then...when Clair show me picture, I go off to calm down."

"Deon, I don't want you to be out on your own."

"Oh, David, I need alone. I know you fear. But I go...uh...so crazy tied in. I like to at least believe I am free, without leash."

"So, where exactly are you?"

"I come back from statue of your President Lincoln. You think one day big statue of President David Asher on park?"

David sounded as if he was either stifling a laugh or a choke of disbelief. "Uh...no. But I am in my car right now. Can I pick you up, or do you have someplace to be."

"Pick up." Deon stopped and looked around to see where he was. "I am just coming to Seventeenth Southwest. Yes?"

"Near the War Memorial?"

"Yes. But not there yet. Is far walk."

"I'll be in a black sedan waiting."

"Yes. Good. I am hot. Is so humid."

"I know. Summers here suck."

Deon smiled. "You talk like real man. Yes?"

"I save the diplomatic jargon for the press. I think my lion can handle the real me."

Deon began to laugh loudly and looked towards the street. "How we keep doing this? Hmm? We must be so crazy."

"Yes. We must. I'm worried about you. I don't want to hang up until I see you."

"So sweet. You fear for me. I am lion, no lamb. I know you think since I make allow for what happen in restaurant, I am helpless. Yes?"

"No. Never."

Deon looked at the people as he walked and talked on the phone, getting closer to the street where David said he would be. "I think fight. Yes. Believe me. But I think first, if no fight, crazy man will no do nothing to harm you. Then I see, of course there is two to battle. And both younger than myself. I no know what they carry. Maybe knife, maybe gun?"

"Deon, you do not need to make excuses to me."

"But, I feel I must. You see me as helpless. I no helpless." He was pushed hard from behind and spun around. It was not an accidental bump. Deon saw a group of younger men, wearing baggie shorts, some carrying skateboards, laughing at him.

Deon quickly pointed his phone at them and took their photo. They gave him the finger and a few tugged their hoodies down to cover their faces.

"Deon?"

Deon could hear David trying to call to him. Deon watched the men. A few kept walking. Two did not.

A cold chill washed up Deon's spine. "David."

"Are you almost here? Where are you?"

"I think…I think young men I just speak of. They are right here."

"What?" David yelled.

Deon tried to take another photo but the two who were lingering turned their backs to him and slipped behind a crowd of tourists.

~

David lunged for the back door of the sedan and began looking for Deon as his guard/driver, panicked and jumped out.

"Deon! Where are you?" The phone to his ear, David began running along the wide cement path, trying not to bump into the hordes of tourists. "Goddamn it, Deon!"

"Sir?" his driver yelled and David heard his footsteps keeping up.

David spotted Deon, his back facing him, staring towards the Lincoln Memorial.

When David approached, Deon jumped and pulled back to punch David, then lowered his arm.

"Where?" David asked, his guard catching up to him.

"I lose in too much crowd. I took photo." Deon scanned the pictures and showed David.

David studied the picture of a group of white kids, wearing hoodies in the heat, low cut shorts, cut below their knees, and tennis shoes, carrying skateboards. Some had their faces completely obscured by sunglasses and the hoods up.

He pointed to the photo. "One of these kids was at the restaurant? The one who attacked you?"

Deon wiped at his brow and said, "I no can think. I need sit."

David held onto Deon's arm and he and his driver walked to the parked sedan. David was furious and worried sick.

A few people pointed at them and he even heard someone ask, "Is that Senator David Asher? The man who is running for president?"

The driver opened the back door and David let Deon climb in first, then sat beside him. The driver turned on the car, cranking up the A/C and David said, "Get us out of here."

"Yes, sir. Anywhere in particular?"

Against his better judgment David said, "My place."

Deon looked out of the window, fanning his shirt as if he were boiling.

Still holding Deon's phone, David studied the photo. It was slightly blurry but the clothing was very distinct. Typical late teen attire, trying to look tough but only would have bravado in a group. David figured if he caught one, he could make him squeal like a pig.

The phone buzzed.

David handed it to Deon.

He answered in French and his voice rose as if he was arguing. David pointed an overhead air vent at himself since he was drenched in sweat and worried sick.

As Deon became animated, throwing up his hand and shouting, David wondered why life was so complex. *Look at us. A fucking fashion model and a senator, powerless to fight some geek punk?*

"*Oui! Oui...*" Deon hung up and held the phone.

"Should I ask?" David leaned on his shoulder.

"Is Clair, assistant. She went crazy when I walk off. She say I need trim, I need this, I need that." Deon muttered in French and David could only imagine the profanity.

"Do I need to drop you off to see her?"

"No. Later. I have show later. I need be..." Deon looked at David. "Need be with you now. For bit."

"Until when?" David touched Deon's hand and Deon immediately interlaced their fingers to hold it.

"I have fashion show at Convention Center. Clair want me there early since show starts at eight. But she also say now I must be at Capital Hilton for dinner. I no want now dinner with strangers. I need private moment. Alone with you."

David immediately became on edge and wanted to go with him to make sure Deon was safe. "I want you guarded. Why did you walk off like that?"

Deon exhaled loudly. "You see lion?" Deon gestured to himself with his free hand. "Lion no need cage!"

"Okay." David clasped Deon's hand in both of his. "I know. I get it."

Deon calmed down and David could feel the heat coming from him from both his anger and the hot walk he had taken outdoors. He turned the vent towards Deon and it made Deon laugh.

"I do not smell nice. No."

David stuck his nose into Deon's neck playfully and sniffed. "Grrr."

Deon began to laugh and David was happy to make him smile. But he kept thinking about that group of brats in the photo. They had to be watching Deon. There was no way they would have known where he was. Not on an unplanned walk at the National Mall.

Thoughts of getting the photo analyzed by his security staff, of using the state's data base, all these things went through David's mind. Military training, tactical planning, using advanced technology. But...

He could not spend taxpayer money on his 'lover'. And using his own? The scandal would sink him.

And if Eric knew where he was right now? After the lecturing he had received from his entire staff this morning to stay the hell away from 'toxic Deon Gael'? They would all go ballistic.

It wasn't a meeting this morning. It was six of his staff members showing him warnings from the internet about the freak who was stalking Deon. Of them telling David, kiss the candidacy goodbye if he gets involved in a sex scandal mess.

David never did go with the flow. He wasn't a sheep. He was the leader. And no one had the right to tell him who he could spend time with. No one!

~

Deon took his first look at the lovely home David owned.

Pointing his finger, David instructed the driver, "Pull up close to the door. Then get out, open my front door, then the car door." He handed the man his key.

"Yes, sir."

Deon kept quiet, waiting. The car pulled right up to the front steps, and the uniformed, armed man, opened the front door, then jogged towards the car and opened the back sedan door, returning the key.

David said to Deon, "Lower your head and get the hell in the house."

"Yes."

David nudged Deon to go first, then was behind him so quickly, he was nearly on Deon's back and into the home in seconds. David looked around the spacious entryway and listened.

Deon kept quiet. It was as if David did not live alone and was trying to determine if he was.

David turned around and opened the front door. He said to the guard, "Stay at right there. I don't care if it's the fucking Vice President himself, no one comes in without you clearing it with me."

"Yes, sir." He was saluted and the young man stood by the entry.

Deon took that moment to investigate the home. It was light and airy, spotless, and had high ceilings. He wandered in just enough to see into the kitchen/dining/ living room area and was impressed with the appeal of the clean lines and uncluttered space.

David touched Deon's shoulder and coaxed him down a long white tiled hallway. David gestured for Deon to enter a room.

A massive master bedroom suite with an attached bathroom appeared. Deon took it in and felt the cool air conditioning with relief. "May I speak?" he whispered.

"Yes." David laughed as he emptied his pockets of his wallet and phone onto a dresser. "I just sometimes have 'guests'." He used air quotes. "Eric, my chief of staff, and even my daughter and son occasionally pop in."

"You have children?" Deon had not recalled hearing about them. But that didn't mean David had not mentioned it. Lately Deon felt as if he were not thinking clearly.

"Yes, two. Both in college." David took off his shirt and tossed it on a chair.

Deon watched him approach, a look of sexy longing in his eyes. David draped his arms over Deon's shoulders and asked against Deon's lips, "Wanna shower with me?"

"You make skin tingle." Deon smiled and touched the hair on David's chest, loving it.

"I'll do more than make you tingle, I'll make you come." David began kissing Deon's neck and earlobe.

Deon closed his eyes and held onto David. "That is given. Yes?"

David began opening the buttons of Deon's shirt. Deon allowed David to undress him. "You have beautiful hands."

David laughed and tossed Deon's shirt over his own. "You should have seen them when I was in the army." He went for Deon's trouser button next.

"Military service. What have you not done?" Deon stepped out of his shoes and slacks.

"Let you fuck me." David tossed Deon's pants aside and backed Deon up to the wall.

Deon felt a surge to his groin at the sexy talk, and ran his hands over David's broad shoulders and chest, running up and down his solid build.

"You want to fuck me?" David teethed Deon's ear teasingly, his puff of a breath making Deon tingle.

"More than you know." Deon reached between David's legs and felt where he had grown hard. He stroked it gently and David began chewing on Deon's neck.

"I can't stop thinking about you." David looked down as Deon opened his zipper and exposed David's cock.

"You have not escaped my mind either." Deon ran his fingertips over David's hard length, making it bob and David moan.

Deon pinched David's small dark nipples and David stepped out of his trousers and shoes. With a hand on his ass, Deon was nudged into a large bathroom with white marble floors and counters. The large space also had a double shower stall, with a showerhead on each side, and a massive bathtub, complete with jets for a whirlpool.

"The government give this you?" Deon looked at the gilded fixtures and faucets.

"No. I bought it." David took off his socks and briefs. "They don't give senators houses."

Deon gave David's erect cock an inspection. He smiled wickedly. "In your eyes I see the lion. You are no lamb."

David closed in on him and pressed Deon against the wall, holding his waist. "I will be your lamb."

"I will enjoy you, lion or lamb." Deon cupped David's face and kissed him. David moaned and reached into Deon's briefs.

Deon kept kissing David, continuing to undress, tugging down his briefs and stepping out of them. He paused in their kisses and removed his socks.

Now he and David were both naked. They stood apart to admire each other.

David shook his head and smiled. "A beauty like you can take down an empire."

"Such flattery. Hope it does not take down anything." Deon rested his pelvis on David's and pressed his mouth against David's lips. David hoisted Deon up, and Deon wrapped his legs around David's hips, interlocking his ankles.

When Deon opened his eyes, he caught David staring at their reflection in the mirror.

Deon looked as well, admiring this man's strength and masculinity. "You look like a born leader. Yes?"

"A leader is not born unless you're talking about a monarchy. Believe me. We have queens here, but there aren't any kings." David winked.

Sliding down David's body to stand, Deon began kissing his way lower, to David's nipples, sucking one then the other. David whimpered and leaned back against the marble double-basin sink counter.

Deon kissed his way down David's treasure trail and then said, "The lion will kneel for his king." He kissed David's cock and then held the base, sucking all of it into his mouth.

"Oh, holy Christ." David gripped Deon's shoulders.

Deon closed his eyes and inhaled the scent of David's body and loved it. He smoothed his hands along David's muscular thighs, then between them. David instantly widened his stance.

Deon held David's soft balls, gently manipulating them in his palm. The sounds of pleasure from David echoed in the tiled room and David began to dig his fingers through Deon's hair, cupping Deon's head and holding it while Deon drew strong suction and moved David's cock inside his mouth from the base to the tip, again and again.

~

David heard both arguments in his head; one from his staff, and one from his daughter. His daughter was winning. And as this incredible man gave him head, David tried to recall the last time he had this kind of sex.

College.

He married Lydia while in graduate-school.

After the divorce, David remained alone.

Suddenly he had one of the most beautiful men he had ever seen, a French runway model, on his knees inside his bathroom, sucking his dick.

And it was sublime.

When Deon wet his finger and began massaging the base of David's cock near his rim, David came. He closed his eyes and clenched his jaw on what was going to be a scream if he did not stifle it. Years of going without had certainly screwed up his staying power, yet at forty-seven, his libido was strong.

Deon hummed and caressed David's body as he swallowed and used his tongue in amazing ways to tickle David's dick inside his mouth.

"Oh, fuck..." David went limp against the sink counter and was surprised his knees didn't give out from the intensity of the rush.

Deon looked up at him with the most devilish grin.

David smiled, then began laughing.

Deon kissed his way back up David's body and met his lips.

Tasting and smelling himself on another's mouth was so foreign to him, it lit him on fire. And Deon's pleasure, enjoying David as if he were still young and vital was more of a stroke to his ego than being urged by his party to join the race to be a presidential candidate.

Deon parted from the kiss and stared at David, the wicked smirk was making David laugh, but he didn't know why.

Deon said, "You ready for lion?"

David suddenly understood why Deon appeared so smug. "Let me get ready."

"I no take your virginity, no." Deon pushed his hard cock against David's spent one.

"Uh, no." David smiled. "But...it has been..." David thought about it. Instead of admitting it was more than twenty years he just said, "A while."

"I allow you time, then we shower?" Deon pointed to the bedroom.

"Sure." David laughed shyly. "There's a well stocked bar in the kitchen/dining area. Why don't you bring us something?"

"I can." Deon pecked David's lips and walked out of the room, looking so sexy it made David moan.

When Deon left, David crouched down and dug under the sink cabinet for what he needed to get himself ready for his lion...in bed.

G. A. HAUSER

Chapter 6

Naked, Deon walked down the long hallway, looking into immaculate bedrooms, all perfectly designed, as if by professionals. He ran his fingertips along the smooth white wall and admired every inch of the home. As he walked by windows he could see each had been carefully covered or shielded by shrubbery, maintaining the senator's privacy. He entered the kitchen and looked around for a liquor cabinet. The room was very light, with a slight Euro-chic flair of glass fronted cabinets, whitewashed like the wooden frames around the doorways, and accented by marble counters.

Lovely.

Enjoying the textures, Deon ran his fingers along the island counter and admired the quality. *Italian marble no doubt.*

He opened a few cabinet doors and then spotted a wet-bar. Standing in front of it, Deon picked up bottles to read labels, and knew his senator was a man of taste and fine breeding. If the government did not pay for the home, David either came from very wealthy parents or had done very well for himself.

Deon poured two glasses of cognac and before he took them back to the bedroom, wanting to give David time to do what he needed for their sex, Deon noticed another hallway in the opposite direction from the bedrooms. He padded lightly down that hall and peered into a study. It was a home office, with a desk and a large black leather swivel chair, a computer with three screens, and walls of reference books on shelves. Then he spotted framed certificates.

Deon approached that wall and read the degrees. Honors, awards, medals, photos of David with heads of countries, and former US presidents…

"*Mon dieu…*"

The admiration Deon had for David filled him with pride.

He kept reading the types of college degrees; law, international relations, government administration…

Then Deon stopped short. David in a military uniform.

"Oh!" Deon touched his lips and caught a scent of David's body off his fingertips. As he inhaled them in delight, he could see David's uniform decorated with medals and stripes, shaking hands with dignitaries, as well as photos of David with a large troop of soldiers. Then he spotted a shadow box contained those medals that had been on David's uniform. There were so many, Deon's eyes began to water from the incredible achievement this man had made throughout his life.

I am so in love with you.

Deon knew the infatuation was partly regarding the actual David that he knew, but this? David the powerful giant of a man?

He kept reading the framed certificates and realized a few were awards for donations, fundraising for veterans, passing laws that had environmental impact of world importance…so his man was not greedy, he was a philanthropist.

Deon began weeping and dabbing at his eyes in awe.

Then Deon stopped to think. Who could wish to harm such a man?

He turned around and there was David, naked, looking confused at the doorway.

Deon wiped at his eyes in embarrassment.

"I thought I lost you." David stepped in slowly. "Why are you crying?"

Deon bit back his emotions. "This." Deon gestured to the wall. "How can there be such a man as this?"

David tilted his head, as if trying to understand.

"How can there be out there someone try to destroy this man?" Deon held his arm out towards the wall of honors.

David closed the gap between them and embraced Deon.

Deon held onto David and was rocked in his arms. "You no deserve this. You no deserve to be smattered with...*merde*..."

"Shh...baby. Don't upset yourself. This is our time. Let's enjoy it."

"Yes." Deon nodded and stood with his back straight. "Our time," he said with resolve.

"I'm ready for my lion." David grinned devilishly.

Deon smiled through his sadness and asked, "We play in shower?"

"Oh, yes." David held Deon around his waist as he walked back down the hallway. "I see you poured drinks. Do you want them?"

"Cognac. We bring to toast...after." Deon smiled.

"Perfect." David picked them up as he walked by the kitchen.

"You have beautiful home, David."

"Yeah?" David carried both glasses to the bedroom, setting them on the nightstand. "You think you could ever live here?"

Deon blinked and laughed as if it was a joke. "Live here? In this house? How would look?"

"Don't know." David gestured to the bathroom. "I suppose it would look like you and I have shacked up." He reached into the shower and turned on one of the shower heads, then the other.

"What is 'shack'?"

David scooped Deon up with one arm around Deon's waist and drew him to his body. "That we are in love. And...live together."

Deon blushed, feeling his cheeks heat up. "In love. A man I just meet. You say things to make me feel like special."

David's smile dropped. He ran his hand over Deon's hair. "To me? You are."

Steam began filling the room.

Deon didn't know what to say. A man he met two days ago? A man who was running for the office of president of the United States?

Why was the word 'yes' coming into Deon's head again and again.

David opened the glass door and gestured for Deon to enter the shower.

He did and walked to one of the heads to wet down. "So luxurious. Yes? One for each?"

"I never turned them both on before." David began soaping up, under his arms and chest. "Never had a guest."

"First? Me?" Deon pointed to himself.

"Yes." David washed his genitals.

Deon closed in on him and took the soap. "Why you no let me do that? Hmm?" Deon ran David's soft cock through his soapy hands.

David moaned and reciprocated. "That feels incredible."

"I must use protection, yes?" Deon didn't want to. He had tested negative regularly.

"I assumed so."

"You test?"

"Yes. When I was active...sexually. Negative."

"Yes. I too. Negative. Mean no have," Deon asked, thinking correctly.

"Yes. Means we are not HIV positive."

"Yes. Means clean." He nodded. "Still use?"

Deon could see conflict in David's expression. He instantly stopped asking. "We use. No more topic. Silly to say." Deon began washing his hair.

"It's not that I don't believe you..."

"Uh!" Deon held up his hand. "Topic is done. We do right thing. Later...when I shack here, maybe no."

David started laughing. "Right."

87

They finished scrubbing up, and Deon was feeling slightly strange, as if the talk of rubbers and seeing the amount this man had achieved in his life had somehow ruined the mood.

They rinsed off and David gave Deon a towel, then used one himself stepping out of the shower to dry off.

Deon watched David's body language, getting lost on his fit build. Something hit Deon about David.

His loneliness.

David had not had a male sexual companion in…a long time. He lived in a huge mansion, alone, and was under so much scrutiny, that even dinner with a man created malicious rumors and internet chatter.

Deon was determined not to disappoint this man.

He tossed the towel aside and began to stalk his prey.

~

David thought he had said some stupid things. *Talk of Deon moving in. What crap. I'm an idiot*.

He dried his legs and as he went to put the towel on the rack he noticed in the mirror's reflection, Deon jerking himself off as he stared at David.

David spun around and caught a wicked gleam in Deon's gaze. It made him smile, then chuckle.

Deon used one hand to push David out of the bathroom, towards the bed, as he continued to self-stimulate. "You had better find protection or your lion will consume you without."

David began to laugh loudly at Deon's threat and took a condom and lubrication out of his nightstand, placing them by the two drinks.

Deon tossed the throw pillows off the bed, grabbed the linen bedspread and yanked it nearly off the mattress and then knelt on the bed. "Get here." Deon pointed to the spot in front of him.

David's skin tingled and he knelt, facing Deon.

Deon grabbed David's jaw roughly and snarled, then kissed him like an alpha male.

David melted right down to his toes. He went to hold Deon and Deon batted his arms down. David's chest began to heave with excitement.

"Lamb does nothing. Nothing but obey."

David stared into Deon's blue eyes and could see the power play. In bed? They were equal. Two powerful alpha males.

What happened outside the bedroom didn't matter at the moment.

"Hands and knees." Deon pointed.

Without hesitation, David faced the headboard, on his hands and knees.

Deon forced David to spread his legs wider with slight taps to the inside of David's thighs.

David closed his eyes and his cock grew thick.

The mattress shifted and David hung his head to see where Deon was positioning himself. It was behind him. The condoms and lube were near David's side of the bed, in front of him.

David felt a slap to his ass, hard, which created a loud sound of a palm hitting flesh. He jumped and blinked, not expecting it. His ass cheeks were spread apart and David held his breath. When Deon went for his rim with his mouth and tongue, David gasped and gripped the bedding. This was a first. Even in college no one had ever done this to him.

"Holy shit." David began huffing for air.

Another slap hit his ass.

"Lamb does not speak."

David kept looking at Deon's legs as he knelt behind him, then his ass was licked and a tongue darted in and out of his rim. David felt like he was going to pass out from the thrill.

His ass wet with saliva, Deon pushed his finger inside gently, all the while nipping on David's bottom, sharp little bites that probably left little red marks.

David felt his cock throb and could see it wagging between his legs. He was so starved for this. Dirty play. How could a man in his position in life enjoy doing things in bed some would think was taboo, beneath him?

More. More.

David imagined Deon doing nasty things to him; tired of being the good boy, the perfect candidate, the celibate homosexual.

The bed shifted.

David watched Deon. Deon moved David's head so he was looking at the bed.

"I no tell you to look at me."

David closed his eyes and waited. He heard the rustle of fabric and couldn't imagine what Deon was doing. David tried to peek but Deon wagged his finger in admonishment.

When Deon began tying David's wrists with a belt David was stunned. "What are you—"

"You want lion or lamb?" Deon asked.

David swallowed down a dry throat. He wanted the lion but it felt humiliating to ask for it.

Deon didn't wait for an answer. He used the belt to bind David's wrists together, then pushed his neck from behind so David's forehead was resting on the leather on his hands and his ass was now high in the air. David interlaced his fingers and closed his eyes, trying not to hyperventilate. This wasn't something he planned for or expected. But it was so damn hot he wasn't going to object.

Playing submissive? Me? To a model?

The thought brought a wicked smile to David's mouth. *About fucking time, Asher. About fucking time.*

The bed moved under him and David didn't try to look this time. He felt Deon push his knees farther apart, making David straddle as wide as he could. Rustling noises followed, and David rested his forehead on the leather belt.

A light touch of slick gel circled his ass.

In order not to make a noise or moan, David bit the leather of the belt, clenching his teeth.

For the first time since college, someone penetrated his ass.

David felt chills rush up his spine and chewed on the leather as his cock began to bounce and hit the bed under him.

"Oh, I think you like the lion."

Oh hell yeah. Oh my fucking God!

"Look at that cock. Hmm? Look how interested he is." Deon stroked it and David was about to come.

Deon began to explore, moving his finger deeper. David nearly hit his head on the headboard when Deon found a sweet spot inside his body.

"There it is." Deon sounded smug. "We find my lamb's pleasure place."

David, with his eyes closed, began to feel as if he were in some surreal dream. How did he find this man? How did he manage to get him to his house? And how did he end up tied up on his bed about to get fucked, and fucked good?

David never imagined this happening. He figured with his position, his family, his staff, and his age, that his sex life was going to be his fantasies or the gay porn on cable TV.

As David got used to the penetration, he realized Deon was using more than one finger. But he also knew, it was not his cock.

"Look how nice, hmm? A massage." Deon rubbed over David's prostate and David felt the urge to come. Wanting to warn Deon he may, David bit down on the leather and tried to hold back. But he had never felt this sensation before. Sure he'd been fucked by a frat boy in law school, but they were both nervous and inexperienced. Mr Gael was neither. He indeed was a lion.

The sensation stopped and David opened his eyes. When he peeked, he spotted Deon enter the bathroom. David tried to think, and assumed maybe he was washing his hands, but the sink never turned on.

When Deon returned David spotted something in his hand, but when Deon realized David was looking, he hid it behind his back and warned, "No you look!"

David wanted to ask, *What is that?*

The bed shifted and something, inanimate, not warm, not Deon, was being pushed into his bottom. David did not own a dildo so he was bewildered since it certainly felt like one.

The item was gently pushed in and out of his ass.

David was about to ask what the hell it was, when Deon slapped his rump with a crack.

The abrupt act made David jump and he shut his mouth and tried to think of what he had in his bathroom that was shaped like a dildo.

"We stretch you out, yes?" Deon pushed something deeper into David.

David bit back a groan and closed his eyes, resting his head again.

"Relax body...so soft, like you are floating." Deon petted David's bottom and pushed the object in and out gently.

David inhaled and rested his cheek on his hands.

"Now we have you ready." The bed shifted again and David waited. He heard something drop to the floor and spotted his hairbrush. The handle was smooth and phallic shaped. He had been fucked by his brush.

This time there was no mistaking a cock was pushing into his ass. Warm, hard and bigger than what had just been inside him.

"My dick. It looks good in your ass, yes?"

David wished he could see it. He said nothing and imagined it.

Deon began pushing deeper, rocking in and out. The heat and friction hit David's sweet spot again and his cock responded.

As David's body allowed Deon to penetrate easily, and the lubrication was smooth as silk, David began moving in time with Deon's rhythm.

"Now, my lamb, let me hear your pleasure."

"Oh, thank fuck." David groaned. "Fuck me! Fuck me, you gorgeous bastard!"

Deon held David's hips and began screwing him hard and fast, their sweaty skin slapping together.

David started to go into a deep swoon, and the internal heat was making his fists clench and his eyes close. "Fuck! Fuck!" David could feel Deon's balls with each thrust, touching his skin. The image in his head of their sex, the intensity of the internal friction and the feeling of being a sub was making David dizzy.

He gasped and could not believe he was about to climax.

Deon's cock throbbed strongly and David sensed, he too, was about to reach the orgasmic high.

When the sensation of a powerful climax began to hit David he was so stunned he choked and punched his fists into the headboard. "Holy fuck!"

Deon gripped him tighter and hammered into David, their bodies uniting like one unit of pure carnal pleasure.

He heard Deon's orgasmic moans as David came at the same time, stunned since nothing was touching his cock. He grunted and jerked his body forward as if he was jamming it into someone but nothing was there but the bed.

Deon moaned and slid in and out of David more slowly, his cock pulsating and David feeling every throb of it deep inside him.

Deon finally pulled out and said, "My lover."

David slipped his hands easily out of the belt and rolled over, the two of them were drenched in perspiration.

Deon caught his breath and was flushed from the body rush and his cock was still hard in the condom.

David felt his own heart racing and stared at Deon as if he were a god. With tears of pure joy about to run from David's eyes, he sprang up and grabbed Deon's jaw and kissed him, embracing him, feeling Deon's sweat, his muscular body and his scent driving David crazy.

Deon kissed back, fervently, touching David all over; his neck, his back, his shoulders. Between their kisses Deon moaned, "Is madness…is madness."

David opened his mouth wider and closed his eyes, lost, hopelessly lost and falling in love.

They groaned as they kissed and finally both men had to gasp for air. They parted and stared at each other as if the most amazing thing on earth had just happened.

"Deon." David was stunned, his jaw dropped but he couldn't find the words to say what he was feeling.

"David." Deon smiled but he appeared exhausted.

David wanted to tell him it was the best fuck he had ever had. He wanted to propose, he wanted to beg Deon to be his, insanity, like a young boy with a teenage infatuation filled with ridiculous lust.

"David?" a deep voice came from the front of the house.

David heard his guard say, "Sorry, Mr Sutten. Senator Asher gave me strict orders."

David grabbed Deon and pushed him towards the bathroom. Deon appeared panicked.

"It's my chief of staff." David grabbed at his clothing that was spread out on the floor.

"David!" Eric yelled, as if the guard was truly trying to keep him out.

"Stay here." David tried to calm Deon down. "Just wash up, dress, and stay here."

Deon nodded.

David pulled his pants on and then his shirt, running down the hall, knowing he looked and most likely smelled of hot sex.

He zippered his pants, tried to button his shirt and tuck it in as Eric sounded furious confronting the security guard.

David tried to smooth his hair and slowed down, walking to the foyer. The guard was literally blocking the way and Eric, appeared about to hit the young man with his walking stick.

When Eric spotted David, he said, "What's this young man trying to do?"

"It's okay." David waved at the terrified guard, who had done an outstanding job considering he was dealing with a man as formidable as Eric Sutten.

The guard stepped aside and Eric entered the house, looking stern. He gave David an inspection as the guard closed the door behind him.

Immediately resenting having given Eric a key, David ran his hand over his hair again. "What do you want?"

"Please don't tell me he's here!" Eric took a step closer to David.

"Eric..." David held out his hand in warning. "Leave. Just go."

"Tell me at least it is not that toxic model. I don't care if you have another man here."

David bristled and pointed his finger at Eric. "Don't you ever use that phrase again."

Eric fumbled with his pockets and took out his phone.

David put his hands on his hips and was still recuperating from the mind-blowing fucking he had just experienced.

Eric showed David his phone as if trying to terrify David into complying. "Read this!"

"No." David took a step back.

"David."

"Eric!" David crossed his arms. "I am not letting some pinhead tell me who I can date!"

"David! It's not a tweet or twit or twart! It's the Sufering Post!"

David shivered and could see on the phone what appeared to be an article from the newspaper's online edition.

Eric narrowed his eyes at David. "You truly don't want to know?"

"What? Know what? A smear campaign against a good man? Huh? Someone trying to derail my bid for presidency? More lies? No. No, Eric, I don't."

Eric stepped closer and David moved back, hitting a wall. He reached for it and could see the warning of his demise in Eric's glare.

"At least read the headline."

"Why? Huh? It will mean nothing to me."

Eric turned the phone towards himself. Put his reading glasses on and said, *"French Model Deon Gael, Offers His Cock For a Price."* Eric looked up at David, who did not react. Eric kept reading, *"The French runway model allows employees of hotels to suck him for a fee, says one source, supplementing his already huge income like a paid gigolo."*

"It's bullshit." David became enraged.

"Don't you see?" Eric took off his glasses and put them back in his shirt pocket. "It doesn't matter if it's true. You don't want to be associated with him. Why can't you hear what all of us said to you this morning? As a group, remember? A few hours ago? David? Are you losing your grip of reality?"

"Go." David pointed to the door.

"David."

"Eric. Go, or I will have the guard escort you out."

Eric appeared to be furious. "You're a fool. You will be the new laughing stock of Washington, David. The next sex scandal. Just wait. By tomorrow? You'll be in the headlines. And I don't want to be the one you call for damage control. You're on your own." Eric used his walking stick and tapped the door.

The guard opened it from the outside and Eric didn't look back as he left.

David stood in the foyer and tried to think, but he couldn't. His mind had hit overload.

He stared into space and sank emotionally, trying to fathom why, when he just met the man of his dreams, did someone come out of the slime of the earth to kill them.

Chapter 7

Deon had washed and dressed in the bathroom. He made sure he was presentable, and then against David's wishes, he left the bathroom. He heard shouting coming from the front of the house and tried to quickly straighten the room in case the man who was yelling loudly decided to search the premise. Deon picked up the brush, the condom wrapper, stuffed the lubrication and condom box back into the drawer, and entered the bathroom to clean the brush and dispose of the condom wrapper. He then picked up the remainder of David's clothing, folded it neatly, made the bed, and stood still, huffing for air nervously. His phone hummed with a text message and he checked the time. Soon he would be expected to attend a dinner at the Hilton. He spotted the glasses of cognac and drank one down quickly.

Once he did, he began moving closer to the hall so he could hear. And what he heard devastated him.

He checked his phone and Clair had texted him, '*you get paid for blowjobs?*'

Deon felt sick and tried to search on his phone for where this source of information was coming from. He found a newspaper and read the headline and article. Deon shook his head in agony. "No...no..." He texted Clair. '*slander! sue this news-rag!*'

When his phone rang he rushed to the bathroom and closed the door, then heard the front door of the house shut loudly.

Deon said to Clair, "Of course I do not do this! You call the editor and get me an apology. A retraction! This is impossible to tolerate!"

"Where are you? Do you know you have all of our contacts here going out of their minds? You left the salon. To go where? You don't answer the texts, the phone. You have an image, Deon! You model for the top lines of Paris! Why are you doing this?"

"Why am I doing this? I?" he began to shout, "I do nothing! I am being targeted by a crazy person! You! You and the staff should call and make the allegations go away."

In a controlled voice, Clair asked, "Where are you?"

"Don't worry. I will be at the hotel dinner. You just call this newspaper. Make calls! If I have to I will contact a lawyer."

"You are with him. Where? He has a home here?"

"Clair, this is my life. My life! You own my work, not my private life." Deon looked up when the bathroom door opened.

David was there, looking worn out. The minute they met eyes, David said, "I'll use a different bathroom," and began walking away.

Deon grabbed him and shook his head, nudging him to the sink and walking to the bedroom. He could see the second cognac glass was empty. "Clair, I will meet you at the hotel lobby for dinner. Yes? In the meanwhile, you call a Washington lawyer. I will sue for slander. Do you understand? You think I will tolerate this slap to my name?"

"Fine. Yes. I will find one. You are right. You are the victim."

"Yes!" Deon said in English so David could understand him, throwing up his free hand. "Victim! Thank you. Now you tell newspaper trash to take away! Take away or face Deon Gael in courtroom!"

"Okay. Yes. I'll see you at the dinner."

Deon disconnected the phone and was so angry he could not think or speak. He stared at the hallway and gripped his phone, wishing he had power. Power enough to stop this menace. Power in a country that was not his. He needed help.

With those thoughts in his head, Deon spun around. David was dressing quietly, putting on his slacks and a dress shirt after washing up quickly.

"David."

David looked up at Deon as he tucked his shirt into his pants.

"You must help."

"What do you want me to do?" David picked up the belt and replaced it in his pants, threading it through the loops.

"I need lawyer to fight slanderous words."

David nodded. He checked his watch. "Saturday afternoon…"

"Nothing? Nothing until work day?"

David sat down to put on his socks. "I have a lot of personal contacts I can call, but I need to figure one out who will be discreet, whom I trust."

Deon suddenly thought about it. He closed his eyes in defeat. "No can come from you." He couldn't believe the irony. One of the most powerful men in the Washington DC and David could not help or be indicated in the scandal.

Deon nodded and began walking out of the bedroom.

"Hang on," David called out to him.

Deon didn't stop, looking at his phone to call for one of the drivers from the modeling agency to pick him up. He felt a hand on his shoulder.

"Wait. Let me just look through my phone numbers and think for a minute. This shit with Eric and the newspaper," David met Deon's eyes, "Which is what we are talking about suing for slander, correct?"

"Yes."

David nodded, and said, "Give me a minute. Okay?"

Again, Deon checked the time on his phone. He had two hours before he had to be at the dinner, and needed to change his clothing and his attitude.

David held out his hand to him. Deon took it. They walked down the long hallway to the office.

David released Deon's hand and sat at his desk, opening a drawer and taking out a leather-bound personal planner. While David was occupied, Deon was drawn to the wall of degrees and honors. He stood before the glass shadow box of medals and then looked at the insignias on David's military uniform. He had no idea what they meant, but they appeared important. "David?"

"Hmm?" David was scanning pages of his notebook.

"What level you in military?"

"You mean rank?" David looked up.

Deon pointed to the picture on the wall. "*Trois étoiles*."

"I don't know what that means."

Deon held up three fingers. "Three. You have symbol with three...star...*oui*. Star."

"Lieutenant General." David picked up the phone on his desk.

"Is high? *Officiers supérieurs?*"

David appeared confused and then said into the phone, "Nick? It's David. Am I calling at a bad time?"

Deon moved closer to the desk, looking down at the files and computer keyboard and screens.

~

"David! What a surprise. Congratulations on your announcement to run for president. I can't wait for the debates to begin."

That was suddenly the last thing on David's mind. "Nick, are you in a position to speak to me in confidence?"

"Well, I'm home, working at my desk. No one is in the room, and unless the government is listening," he chuckled, "you have my word."

David waved for Deon to sit down on a chair across from him since Deon appeared so nervous. Deon did and folded his hands on his lap.

"Nick, I don't know if you keep up on some of the internet trash…"

"I try not to. I avoid it like the plague. Why? Has something come up?"

David wished Nick knew. He rubbed his face tiredly. "Unfortunately."

"What? Christ, David, you have a spotless record, you're a war hero, and are out. What could anyone say in the crappy world of internet bullshit about you?"

"Well…it's not about me directly." David met Deon's eyes.

"Okay…" Nick said slowly.

"I…I met a man…and well…"

"I'm listening."

"His name is Deon Gael. He's a French fashion model. We met at a fundraiser just the other day."

"So? You are free to date. Are you afraid being seen with a handsome man will upset your constituents?"

"It's more complicated than that. Ever since I met Deon he has become the victim of a stalker. Some crazed loon who seems to have enough savvy to smear this man everywhere from Twitter to The Sufering Post."

"And? What does this have to do with you?"

"Well." David stared directly into Deon's blue eyes. "I'm dating him. And my chief of staff is going crazy thinking this will derail my campaign chances."

"What type of things are they saying?"

"He is right here. Can I put him on?"

"Of course."

"And, Nick. Thank you. I know I can count on your discretion. If the media or this nut case knew I was referring you to him, it may appear unsavory. You know?"

"Trust me."

"I do. That's why I called you. Here's Deon." David handed him the phone. "Nick Backus. He's a great attorney."

Deon nodded and took the cordless phone. "Hello?"

David rocked in the leather chair as he listened to Deon's side of the conversation.

"*Oui.* Yes, it began strangely. He pretend to be hotel employee. Yes? He gain access to room. Made sexual advance."

David wouldn't have been furious a few days ago that Deon had touched another man. But things felt as if they had shifted. David knew it was insane, but he wanted exclusivity with this man. Starting now.

"Yes…that is when began. He post photo. And in shower!" Deon grew animated. "Shower photo appear. I was mortify." Deon nodded and David grew more enraged.

"Now David get notify a newspaper write terrible thing. They claim I am paid whore!" Deon muttered something in French under his breath then appeared to be listening.

David stood from the desk and rubbed his face and the back of his neck. The more he heard the more his rage became unbearable.

"Yes! I want retract! Apology! I have spotless reputation. I need keep very good record. I work with top names in Paris." Deon ran his hand over his hair as he spoke. "This is complete outrage. What if my work is jeopardize?"

David clenched his fists and needed to find this punk.

"Yes." Deon nodded. "Of course. I authorize you call on my behalf. Yes." Deon nodded with more conviction. "You tell them to prove! To name person whom I did this. Who they say exchange money for act."

David left the room. He was so angry he was about to combust. He paced in the kitchen for a few minutes, still hearing Deon's voice but no longer his words.

David kept asking himself what more he could do. What he wanted was to be seen with Deon. Show the world Deon was worthy of being his partner and not to believe the lies and slander being spouted.

David began composing speeches and letters in his head about bullying, internet harassment, and the ruin of a man's integrity by the anonymity of the disgusting websites.

Deon appeared from the hall, holding the phone. "He want speak."

David took the phone. "I'm here."

"I'm looking up the article and internet garbage. I can't believe the deliberate smear campaign on this poor guy. What the hell, David?"

"I know." David watched Deon turn away, as if he wanted to allow David privacy. "Nick, I am so furious I am ready to kill."

"David, that's exactly what this punk wants. He wants you to be so enraged that your competition can nail you for it in a debate. You know this is all a way to derail you."

"So, you think this was perpetrated by one of my competitors? Someone in my party who is trying to get the nomination?"

"What other motive can there be? This guy is French. Odds are the people in his own country won't even figure out what's going on. And even though it appears to be against Deon, when did it begin, David?"

"When we met." David was crushed. "I feel helpless. It's as if the more I fight for Deon the worse both of us will appear."

"What does Eric Sutten advise?"

David stifled a choke of fury. "He…" He walked away from Deon so Deon could not hear, back to his office and shut the door. "He said Deon is now toxic and I need to not be seen with him."

"Well…"

"Nick." David stared down at his computer keyboard and tried to calm down. "I really like this guy."

"Enough to fuck up your hopes at being the next president?"

"God!" David balled his fists and looked up at the ceiling. "I am about to explode."

"Calm down. Look. Let me call the fucking paper. I am now Deon's legal representation. I will threaten them with a million dollar lawsuit if they don't retract and apologize immediately. So let me handle it."

"I want to pay you."

"David, don't be foolish. Deon can pay me. If they trace your account and you are buying this man's attorney?"

"Fine. Whatever. Now how do I get my hands around the throat of this fucking asshole?"

"I told Deon I will hire a private investigator. David, do not hire anyone yourself. Let me do it."

"And?" David asked, "Is your advice to me going to be the same as Eric's? Stay away from this man?"

"In public, yes. And if this freak is stalking Deon? Then even in private you are risking your political future."

"I can't believe this!" David said, "This is the first man I have had a date with since college!"

"I'm sorry, David. You chose the most high profile position for a political politician possible. You know every candidate will be under the magnifying glass."

"Fuck!" David bit his lip. "I'm sorry, Nick. I'm sorry I said that."

"Uh, David, I've heard the word before, and I get your frustration."

"So…" David inhaled and straightened his back. "I have two choices; stay away from a man I am crazy about or chance going out with him and losing my support for president."

"In a nutshell? Yes."

"Fine."

"Let me call the fucking editor of this rag now. I hate this shit."

"Good. Yes. Thanks, Nick. Can you keep me in the loop?"

"No. But I will make sure Deon knows it all. It's now client attorney privilege, David, and even though we are friends, I can't do that."

David nodded. "I understand. Thank you."

"I'll squash it. Don't worry."

"Thanks." David hung up and tried to calm down.

~

Deon could hear David's anger through the door.

He sighed loudly and moved to sit in the living room, sinking into a soft sectional sofa and resting his head back on the cushion. He closed his eyes and tried to stop his anger. The lovemaking was so wonderful, and now all the warmth was gone. Vanished.

Deon put his hands behind his head and tried to think it through. *How would it work? I am in Paris, he is here...my work makes me travel all around the globe, he stays in DC...there is nothing here to hold onto.* He rubbed his eyes and muttered to himself in French, "Yet we torture ourselves over this nightmare."

The office door opened and Deon looked up from where he was sitting, over the back of the couch, towards the hall. David stood behind him, massaging his shoulders affectionately.

"Can you afford a lawyer?"

"Yes. Of course." Deon felt David press his lips to the top of his head. Deon reached backwards to touch him. "We struggle so hard for a love affair that is finite. I no live here, you can no live in Paris? Yet we suffer cruelly."

"I have quite a few breaks during the year. I can go to Paris." David joined Deon on the couch and placed his hand on Deon's thigh. "If you wanted me to."

"How can you? While president?"

David smiled and turned his body to face Deon, in contact with him from their shoulders to their knees. "I may not get the nomination. Many of my party members want to be selected."

"I no understand U.S. politics."

"It's complicated, but not rocket science. I'd explain it but I'd put you to sleep." David touched the soft hair of Deon's sideburn. "And we never got to bask in the afterglow of that amazing sex."

Deon smiled as David's expression changed completely. "We no get to bask. What is bask?"

"Savor."

"Yes. I think that is meaning. Would like to have stayed in bed and held to you." Deon ran his hand down David's leg. "But the world does not want us to bask." Deon shrugged. "How we have effect on so many, I have no idea why. We simple two men who love."

David laughed. "Simple. Just two men."

"In real world. Yes. In outside." Deon gestured to the front of the house. "They see different. They see fashion model and president for future. Not simply men who love."

"You're right. And I really believe if this idiot who is either jealous of me dating you, or out to ruin my chance at the White House had not shown up, you and I would have been...just two men, together."

"This so? You think?"

David shrugged, caressing Deon's hair with his fingertips. "I'm out. You're out. And other than some interest in us being on a date together, I don't think much more would have mattered."

Deon thought about it carefully. "Then...if simple just two men together, and already press is out that I am 'oh-such-a-whore!'" Deon waved his hand expressively. "Then is still not just two men? If we defy? We no let this stranger dictate?"

David's smile faded and he too appeared pensive.

"Two powerful lions?" Deon asked, "Me. You. Allow an insect to decide our fate?"

David shifted to face forward on the sofa, interlacing his fingers on his lap. Deon could see the wheels spinning in his head.

Deon leaned his chin on David's shoulder. "Have you been the kind of man to listen to others' instruction?"

"Hardly." David made a noise of disbelief in his throat.

"Your staff, the man who yell at you, he tell you and you obey?"

The corners of David's lips curled in a slight smile. "Eric. Well, he has known me since I was a baby. He was very close with my father."

"So, yes. You obey him like father."

"No." David chuckled. "I think that frustrates Eric. He probably knows best, and with his help and the help of my entire staff, I am in a very good position to win the nomination of my party."

Deon struggled to understand but got the gist of what David was saying. "So, we allow insect or we no allow."

David's expression became stern. He gripped Deon's hand and said, "We don't allow."

Deon purred and whispered in his ear, "That is my lion."

David spun around and grabbed Deon by his jaw, kissing him and lying on top of him.

Deon felt the weight of David's body in pleasure and knew, good wins. And this nasty creature will be sued, and exposed. Right?

David parted from the kiss breathlessly and asked, "Can I be your date tonight for the dinner?"

Deon laughed. "Yes!"

David pressed him against the sofa and chewed on Deon's jaw, nipping his bottom lip and then using his tongue to enjoy Deon's kiss.

Chapter 8

Deon sat in the backseat of his company's sedan, while David followed behind him with his own security guard/driver.

Before they left David's home, Deon helped David pick out a fabulous designer suit and tied his tie for him. They didn't have sex again but the flirting, kissing and playing, was so much fun for Deon. Deon had also stopped at his hotel to change and prepare for an elegant dinner.

Deon turned in his seat to look out of the back window, seeing the dark sedan and uniformed driver, then he smiled to himself, knowing Clair and his company's staff were in for quite the surprise.

He was in the opposite position as David. Having the man who was potentially going to be the next President of the United States as his date? Well, for Deon, after all the bad publicity, it would simply lay to rest any doubt about his character.

Deon was pleased David had so much love for him he wanted to spend the time they had left together. Deon was going to head back to Paris soon, and even with the busy schedule in Washington, both men were committed to trying to spend their free time wisely. Or...in this case, David certainly found his presidential balls, and decided on his own, he would attend as Deon's date.

Although Deon was slightly on edge, never wanting harm to come to his lover, Deon had no idea how anyone could penetrate the security around this dinner, or his fashion show after. It was invitation only, high-priced, and select individuals who were personally invited to attend. An 'insect' such as the criminal who was slandering him, would never be able to sneak his way in.

Deon peeked back once more at the sedan behind him. *At least I hope this is so.*

~

David brushed lint off his black dress slacks and said into his phone, "Eric, if I tell you where I will be tonight, you will fill my ear with shit."

"Then you are defiant. Determined to play this to the end."

"If you mean, not let a bully and a stalker ruin my chance at a fabulous boyfriend, yes."

"Oh, David. I wish your father were alive."

"Why? I would do the same thing. And as a matter of fact, Dad would get out his hunting rifle and find this jerk."

He actually heard Eric laugh, which made David smile. "You know I'm right."

"You are. Your father had no fear. But he also never ran for president."

"Look, Eric, am I going to show the world I have balls? Or am I going to cower in a corner at the first sign of bad publicity?"

"They know you have balls. You have proven that with your military career. But the fact that you are the only openly gay candidate is already not a plus. You realize even with the wave of decency in this country, legalizing gay marriage in every state, there is still a very strong hard right core."

"I do realize that. And when I have a debate with my competition, I have no doubt this affair with Deon will be brought up."

"Are you ready for that?"

"To what? To defend the fact that I love a gorgeous French model?"

"…love? Did you say you love this man?"

110

David shook his head. "No. I mean, Eric, I'm saying if I am attacked because of my relationship with Deon, won't it appear as if I am being bullied, just as Deon is now?"

"If the public believe Deon is indeed being slandered. Maybe."

"Deon hired a lawyer. The lawyer is going to demand an apology and retraction from the newspaper or he will sue for slander."

"And where did Deon get this lawyer?"

"Eric." David grew weary.

"It doesn't matter what I say. You are determined to be with this man, aren't you?"

"Yes." David could see Deon's sedan pull into the loop at the hotel's front entrance. "And first we are having dinner at the Hilton, then I am going to his fashion show at the Convention Center after. So?"

"So? I'll tell the staff to prepare for the onslaught of media madness."

"Eric." David felt his car slow to a stop behind Deon's. "We are two men dating. Period."

"Time will tell."

"Goodbye." David hung up and his personal bodyguard opened the back door for him. David stepped out and immediately joined Deon who looked spectacular in his designer suit and tie, and they held hands.

Deon smiled proudly and a doorman opened the glass doors for them as both of the men's personal guards stepped in close behind them.

What David didn't expect was camera flashes from news media the moment he and Deon entered the lobby. David said to his guard, "Get rid of them."

The guards, as a team, pushed back the media and Deon and David kept walking to the extravagant ballroom where the exclusive dinner was being served.

David noticed a young woman standing near the entrance and the minute she spotted Deon she rushed him and began speaking in French, so quickly, David wondered if something was wrong.

Deon nodded, and gestured to David. "David, this is Clair, she is personal assistant. Clair, this is Senator David Asher."

"Senator," she said, smiling shyly. "Is pleasure to have you accompany."

He shook her hand. "My pleasure as well."

"Come this way. I show you where you sit." She led the way into a glittering room with crystal chandeliers, and servers in black attire hustling from table to table.

Deon was shown to a table where a place setting read his name and beside it, '*guest*' was on the card. David looked around the table of people and had no clue who he was dining with.

In French, Clair made some kind of introduction and gestured to David.

Deon said to David, "These are the associates of the designers of the clothing I represent."

"Oh." David waved, nodded politely, and sat down as they greeted him excitedly.

Clair said one more thing, "*Il sera le prochain président américain.*"

Even though David did not speak French, he certainly figured out she was saying he was either running or going to be the next president.

The muttering from the people at the table changed and many brightened up and congratulated him.

"Thank you," David said then asked Deon quietly, "What did she say?"

"She say you will be next president."

"That's not really true." David felt the looks of admiration and smiles and as his cheeks flushed. "As a matter of fact, it could be completely wrong."

Deon laughed. "That is Clair. What can I say?" He placed his napkin on his lap as a server immediately poured water for them.

An older man leaned across the table and asked, "When is the election?"

"November." David sipped the water as the waiter asked Deon, "Do you want something from the bar, sir?"

"No. I have to perform later." Deon shook his head.

David tried not to get distracted.

"How did you meet our charming, Deon?" A lovely woman asked, her neck covered in jewels.

"At the fashion show fundraiser he just did." As the waiter asked him if he wanted a drink, David shook his head no to the alcohol as well.

"Really?" Another woman appeared surprised. "And here you are with our beautiful model. Are you two an item?"

David glanced around and noticed people at other tables talking and looking at them. "I think we are now."

Deon chuckled and placed his hand on David's leg under the cover of the white tablecloth.

"Is acceptable for gay president?" a man with a thick French accent asked, appearing stunned.

"I suppose that's something we're going to find out." David noticed a small placard with the menu choices beside his plate.

"Is very nice! I hope the people choose move forward." A man nodded. "What difference? Hmm? Whom we love in the bedroom."

Deon said, "Precisely. Perhaps America will lead the way with shining light." Deon squeezed David's leg and smiled at him.

David looked at the menu choices. "They all look good."

"Well, is very expensive affair." Deon leaned on David as if reading his menu with him to decide.

David noticed everyone looking at them, smiling like proud parents. It was slightly odd since David had never been out with a man publicly. Not like this. The restaurant they had eaten in previously had a private room. Here? David looked around. There had to be at least two hundred people present.

A server approached and stood waiting for their order.

Deon sat up and said, "The blue cheese wild endive salad, to begin…"

David listened to Deon choices and wondered if it would seem silly to order the same things. But he was making the choices David had picked in his mind.

When the waiter turned to David, he smiled and said, "The same."

The waiter laughed and then said quietly, "Can I just say thank you, Senator? I am so proud to serve you."

David realized, it was a way for this man to tell him he is gay. It wasn't the first time a gay man had thanked him for boldly going where no other out gay man had gone before.

"Thank you. And it's my pleasure to serve my country."

The man actually fanned himself as if he were overwhelmed and walked off.

Deon laughed and said to David, "You are so loved."

"Gay men love me. Of course." David made sure his napkin was still on his lap.

"I know one gay man who does." Deon smiled slyly.

David nudged him with his elbow. "Behave. You actually can't be a bad boy here. These people pay your salary."

"Is true." He sipped the water. "And they will give me their outfits to wear tonight."

"I can't wait." David smiled.

Deon met his gaze and tilted his head in such a way, David knew exactly what Deon wanted. So, he pecked his lips with a light kiss.

A little commotion was heard around them and even clapping.

114

In French, several of the people at the table said something to Deon, which made him appear modest and smile.

David held Deon's hand and exhaled a deep breath. Here, inside the world of fashion, there was no animosity regarding sexual preferences. Like acting and theater, it was a warm and loving environment.

But outside…in some states, states which held powerful political clout, red was the color they favored. And voting for an out gay man? One who was in love with a pretty French model?

It was a long shot.

But David knew Deon was worth it. Yes, he was. If the public accepted David as an out gay man, then they had to understand that meant…he actually loved men.

And seeing Deon in his element, speaking French to his beloved designers, David couldn't imagine why it would make a difference.

But a little voice in his head warned him.

It did.

It was the difference between winning and losing.

~

Deon tried not to eat too much since having a full belly in some of the outfits he was going to model would not look nice. He did not starve himself like some models, especially the women, but Deon also had enough sense to not bloat before a show.

As the group warmed up to them, Deon was happy to see David enjoying himself. Neither of them had their phones on, since in this type of setting it would not only be rude, it was classless.

Clair appeared behind Deon and whispered, "They want you to come to the exhibition hall for a few minutes. There are booths set up with gifts, and David may find some nice things to enjoy for himself."

"Yes. It sounds lovely. I was intending to go." Deon set his napkin on the table and since Clair was speaking in French, he told David, "There is a place I want to take you. In hotel." Deon pointed. "And then I must go prepare for fashion show."

"All right." David smiled and scooted out his chair. He stood and every member of their table reached out to shake David's hand and wish him luck in the election.

David politely made the rounds and thanked them, then noticed other tables of patrons were smiling and tittering about his presence at the dinner.

With Deon escorting him, David made sure he played the diplomat and smiled and nodded as people acknowledged him with supporting smiles and waves.

Clair hurried them down a carpeted hall and the two guards, who had been outside the room chatting together hurried over.

"Sir?" David's guard appeared concerned.

"Everything is fine. I'm just going to another room with Deon."

The man gave him a sly smile.

"No." David knew what the man was thinking. He pointed down the hall. "Not a hotel room." David kept up with Deon and Clair and asked his security guard, "Did you eat?"

"Yes. One of the waiters brought us both a meal." The young uniformed man gestured to Deon's security man as well.

"Good. We are going that way," David pointed, "And then Deon has to prepare for his show, and I will be going to that as well."

"Very good, sir."

David gave his attention back to Deon who smiled in excitement and gestured to an enormous room jammed with people and booths of venders surrounding the perimeter.

The acoustics were lousy and David wasn't a big fan of crowds, especially with someone stalking his lover.

He tilted his head for the security guards to keep close, and they immediately closed the gap behind them.

Deon seemed to be well known in the fashion circles and rushed to kiss both men and women on both cheeks, and was handed gift bags at each booth. Some exchanged conversation with Deon in French, while others used English, excitedly greeting him.

David was not a fashionista by any stretch of the imagination, and usually went shopping with his ex-wife or daughter to make sure he didn't pick out something 'inappropriate'. But most of his meetings he attended he wore a suit and tie, and although David would prefer jeans, he rarely was able to wear them because of his 'potential' to be the country's next leader.

Yet, seeing Deon in his element, like watching him glide the catwalk, was intriguing and gave David a glimpse into another world, one he had never entered.

"David!" Deon waved him over enthusiastically.

Being attentive, David stepped closer to a booth and waited to see what was so exciting about it.

"David! Here. You must have this cologne." Deon held up a small gift bag with tissue paper sticking out of it.

"Okay." David had no idea why he 'must' but Deon seemed very animated as if he had won the lottery. He peered into the small bag and tried to find the cologne.

"David! It is Mark! He is American model fabulous!"

Smiling, still trying to figure out where the cologne was in the paper wrapping, David stopped fussing and looked at an enormous ad for the cologne being used as the backdrop, behind the make-shift counter with several cologne products on it. When he noticed the model on the enormous ad was in fact the man standing behind the counter, wearing a sleek suit jacket over a black crew neck top, David met this man's gaze.

"David! This is world famous Mark Antonious Richfield, yes?" Deon acted as if he were meeting his favorite celebrity. "Mark Antonious! This is Senator David Asher."

Mark extended his hand and smiled. "Well! Very nice indeed to meet the man I am hoping will be the next president."

David tried to find his tongue as this gorgeous man with long thick brown hair, brilliant green eyes, and slight British accent reached to touch him.

David clasped his hand to shake.

Deon held David's arm and squeezed it. "Mark was one of the first top models to come out, yes? So he and you have in common to be first in best things."

David looked at the ad behind Mark -the man- and blushed at the erotic nature of Mark's bare chest and sexy smirk, while posing with a white horse for *Dangereux* Cologne.

"Lovely," Mark said, as he shook David's hand. "Well, I can tell you, Senator, if you get the party nomination, you will have all of Los Angeles on your side. Or at least my mates." Mark laughed.

Although Deon was very handsome, David had never met anyone quite as spectacular as this man.

"You must smell." Deon reached into the bag and removed the little cologne bottle which was inside a small box, one that David had not been able to find.

David released the clasp of Mark's hand and stared at him, then the ad, then noticed on the table several postcards with Mark's photo on it, and tiny sample bottles attached.

"You see." Deon sprayed a little cologne onto his wrist, waved it around before he put his hand under David's nose.

The scent was delicious and David could not get over how beautiful the model was.

"Is fabulous!" Deon sniffed his own wrist. "I must have photo with Mark." Deon dropped the cologne back in the bag David held, and gave David his phone.

David tried not to appear clumsy as Deon leaned towards Mark and Mark leaned closer to Deon over the counter separating them. David held up the phone, could see the image on the screen and took the photo.

Deon immediately reached for the phone and looked at the picture. "Is perfect!"

Mark gave David a wicked smile, as if he knew David found him attractive. "Do you want a photo with me, love?"

"Huh?" David woke out of his daydream state. "No. Unless you want one of me. I mean…"

Mark shrugged. "I wouldn't mind. That way I can say I met our next president." He handed Deon his phone.

Deon nudged David to move closer to Mark.

David felt awkward as Deon acted like a teenager who has met a pop idol. He stood facing Deon, leaning on the counter and felt Mark touch him, putting his arm around his shoulder. David caught the scent of the cologne on this man and his cock moved in his trousers.

"Say cheese!" Deon laughed and took a picture.

David hoped he smiled in time for the flash and felt Mark peck him on the cheek.

"A kiss for luck," Mark whispered.

There was no doubt David's face was red because he was an inferno at the moment.

Deon handed Mark back the camera and waved. "So nice to meet you. You will be at show later?"

"No, lovely. I have to fly back tonight. My new shoot for the car manufacturer is tomorrow. Work, work, work!"

"Is still lovely to meet. You have always been my idol. Yes?"

David watched Mark and Deon kiss on the lips and nearly passed out at seeing those two men kiss so casually, yet it was the hottest thing David had ever witnessed.

"Come! So much more to show." Deon hooked David's arm and began to lead him to the next booth.

David held Mark's gaze and Mark winked at him flirtatiously and then was distracted by the next fan.

Now, in a complete daze, David couldn't think or hear anything as the image of his lover and Mark kissing completely blew him away.

His world was the polar opposite from Deon's…David lived and worked around politicians who would sooner punch each other than show affection. And seeing two men, two men as beautiful as Deon and Mark kiss, had him slightly dizzy, not to mention, hard as hell.

As Deon began to scan the room for the best booths, David discreetly brought Deon's hand to his crotch. The area was packed with people trying to stuff bags full of the samples.

Chapter 9

Feeling David place his hand on his erection, Deon spun around in surprise. The room was over-crowded, and they were pressed close, the two bodyguards behind David. Deon met David's brown eyes and could see something had lit the fire in him.

"We need go to private spot?" Deon whispered.

"You know one?" David glanced around, but the crowd was much more interested in the free gifts than them.

"Will find!" Deon gave David's length a rub and squeeze, then made an about-face and pointed to the exit.

David said something to the two men who were struggling to keep them safe in a room so filled with people.

As David followed the guards, Deon kept close, touching David's bottom and tried to figure out what had made David so excited. Then he passed by the *Dangereux* Cologne booth and realized it had to have been Mark. Mark Antonious, the ultimate aphrodisiac. Deon chuckled to himself and couldn't catch Mark's gaze as Mark signed autographs and posed with his fans.

Getting out of that room, which had gone from slightly crowded to mobbed as the dinner finished, Deon took a breath of air and watched David looking around the area.

"Men's room too low for you?" Deon whispered.

"May be our only option since I'm not exactly going to rent a room." He said something to his security guard that Deon could not hear.

The guard nodded and the four men walked to the restrooms. The guard entered the room and when he came out he said, "Clear, sir."

David nodded. "Make sure no one enters."

Deon blinked in surprise as David opened the door and tried to casually tilt his head for Deon to go first.

Deon gave all their sample bags to his guard and said to him, "No trespass."

The man chuckled, as if he had a good idea what was going on and nodded.

David looked around the moderate-sized men's room and then held Deon's hand taking him to the last stall which was a large handicapped stall.

Deon kept stifling his laugh as David seemed very hot to trot. Once inside the stall, David pushed Deon against the wall and kissed him, bringing Deon's hands to his groin.

Deon quickly opened David's belt and zipper, and before he knelt down, he asked, "Must know. Was it Mark Antonious?"

"It was the two of you kissing." David exposed his stiff length.

Deon smiled knowingly and crouched down, drawing David's cock into his mouth.

David moaned and moved to lean against the wall as Deon scooted to a better position to enjoy David.

~

David kept imagining what having a three-way romp with Deon and Mark Richfield would be like. He was ready to cream his briefs. Closing his eyes he grabbed Deon's head and fucked his mouth, knowing they could not spend too much time in the men's room, and preventing other guests from using it.

He went into an incredible fantasy, the cologne scent of that green-eyed god with the long hair still lingering on Deon's clothing. David felt the sensation of pleasure begin to rush through him and gasped, not saying a word as he came in Deon's mouth.

Deon whimpered and milked David's cock gently, then wiped his saliva off of it and tucked it into David's briefs for him.

As Deon stood, David quickly fastened his pants.

Deon leaned against him and smiled wickedly. "I wish to know what naughty thoughts in your head."

"I'll tell ya later." David grinned and opened the stall to check his reflection in the mirror as Deon washed his hands and also, gave himself a quick look.

"No have your cum on me?" Deon teased.

"Funny man." David grabbed his hand and headed to the door. "Thanks."

"Is my pleasure."

They exited the room and caught their two security guards smirking, as if they knew exactly what had just gone down.

David pretended nothing unusual had happened, although many of his opposing party politicians had men's room dramas of their own.

David said, "Deon needs to get ready for his fashion show."

"Yes, sir."

Deon said, "Is at Convention Center. First I need call Clair to see what needs doing." He removed his phone from his pocket.

David walked behind the two guards as Deon spoke French on the phone.

Once they were near the front entrance, David's driver said, "Sir? Wait here with Deon and his security man while I get your car."

"Good. Thank you." David nodded and his man left.

He stood by as people came and went from the dining room and the vendor hall, and then noticed outside the hotel was a huge gathering of news media, now being kept out of the hotel lobby since the dinner had ended and people were leaving to either go to the fashion show or home.

Deon finished his phone conversation and looked around the crowd.

"Is everything okay?" David asked him.

"Yes. Clair is try to find me. She wants to ride with me."

David nodded and looked for her.

A petite woman waving over the crowd was trying to make her way over to them. Deon noticed her and waved back, letting her know he had seen her.

David checked his watch and when he looked up Deon was nearly pressed to his chest, their lips close.

"Until later?" Deon asked, a slight smirk in his expression, as if he knew he was being naughty.

David could catch the scent of himself on Deon's skin. He backed up and said, "I'll find you."

Clair gestured for Deon to hurry and called to him in French.

"No kiss?" Deon gave him an exaggerated pout.

"Later." David cleared his throat and straightened his tie, looking around at the crowd.

The guard who had gotten his car appeared and said, "Sir?" and gestured to the door.

David approached him and as he did, he and Deon ended up exiting the hotel together.

Flashes of light from the media hit instantly and Deon and Clair moved towards a black sedan parked a few yards away from David's car.

David's security guard tried to keep back the crowd, but microphones were suddenly pushed in front of David's face as reporters asked, "Are you and the French model seeing each other, Senator?"

"Rumor is he is going to be staying at your residence here in DC."

"Senator! Do you think marrying a foreigner will ruin your chances of being selected as the party's candidate?"

David shook his head at the absurdity of the comments and the guard opened the backseat of his sedan for him.

As David sat down, not responding to the media frenzy that had obviously been notified he was attending the dinner, David heard one reporter ask, "Did you pay the man as an escort?"

Before David could react and throw a punch, or at least a scream of fury, the driver closed the door, got in, and got him out of there.

David was breathing fire and finally turned on his phone. It beeped with dozens of missed calls and text messages.

"The Convention Center, sir?"

"Let me stop home first. I don't think I need to be dressed in my best black suit."

"Yes, sir."

David put the phone to his ear. "What now, Eric?"

"I was informed your presence at the dinner at the Hilton has caused a media storm."

"I know. I just weathered it." David looked out of the window as traffic crawled.

"Photographs of the two of you kissing have already hit the social media."

"Kissing?" David tried to think and then realized he and Deon shared a quick peck on the lips at the table. He didn't expect anyone in the room of fashion and high style's chic patrons to stoop that low.

"Do I have to send it to you?"

"No." David rubbed his rough jaw. "Eric...it was just a kiss."

"David...the fodder you are giving your competitors in a debate is ridiculous."

"Oh? A kiss? So if one of them kissed their wife or girlfriend it would be front page news?"

"David..." Eric said like a disapproving father. "Why do I have to keep reminding you of how you are ruining your future?"

David slouched in the backseat and said, "And how can a man who has come out as gay be attacked for kissing a man he really likes?"

"You better be careful that's all they see you do."

"I'm getting very angry, Eric. And not with just the media."

"Look, the internet has become both the boom and the bane of everyone. I am just telling you, everything you are doing right now with this man?"

David thought about the bathroom stall blowjob and knew he never had done anything like it before.

"It's being sent around the world like wildfire. Viral. That photo of you kissing Mr Gael will be on every blog and tweet."

"And why is that bad? Hmm? Eric, the public cannot expect me to be celibate. It's been this way for too long. Christ, I am so fucking starved for affection I explode every time he touches me."

"I don't need to hear this."

"Sorry, but it's true. Okay? What do they expect? Huh? I'm going to suddenly wear a white collar around my neck and be a born again virgin?"

He heard a loud laugh come from his driver, who immediately apologized, "Sorry, sir," and kept quiet.

His chief of staff said, "It's my job to keep you informed, for your staff to do damage control, and for us to keep you on track for your nomination for president. That's all we're trying to do."

"But..." David ran his hand over his hair at his frustration. "If they can accept me as an out gay man, why can't they accept me as a man with a date? With a love life?"

"I don't have the answer to that question. I just know your popularity has dropped in the polls since this mess. Since you met this...this..."

David bristled. "This what, Eric?"

"...man."

"You do realize there are politicians who have had affairs, done dope, embezzled money, lied, cheated…and have been reelected."

"You don't have to tell me. I know."

"Yet…" David was sick of the debate and the driver had pulled up to his home. "Forget it. It's Saturday night, I just had a great dinner with my boyfriend and now I am changing and going to see his fashion show."

"I hope you have someone with you to fend off the media."

"I do, but he's been with me for hours. Time for a changing of the guard to give this man a break."

"I'll send you his relief."

"Thanks." David shut off his phone, ignoring the other messages and calls, and the driver opened his door. David said, "Eric is sending someone to relieve you. Thanks." He extended his hand.

"My pleasure, sir. Oh. And here is your gift bag." He gave David the small bag with the cologne.

"Thank you." David walked to his front door and opened it, then headed to his bedroom and set the small bag down on the nightstand. He sat on his bed and unknotted his tie, wishing he had time for a quick nap, but he did not.

As he changed clothing, he sensed something. He looked around his bedroom and didn't know what was wrong. He took a look around the room, and he couldn't put his finger on it, but it felt as if someone had been in it while he was gone.

And it was not the cleaning staff, since his bed was not made.

David inspected the window, which was locked, and then his dresser. Nothing appeared out of place and he wondered if he was just being paranoid.

He sat back down on the bed to remove his shoes and then noticed the carpet near the air duct had tiny white flakes on it. David stood up, walked closer to the duct and squatted down.

He touched the little chips and could see what it was. Tiny paint flakes. Being in the military and through training which included spotting IEDs, David noticed both screws on the metal duct appeared to have recently been tampered with. He backed up and called the police department's private emergency number so they already knew who was calling.

"Sir?"

"Someone has been in my home while I was gone. I don't know who. Can you send me someone from the bomb squad?"

"Yes, sir! Evacuate the home, Senator."

"I'll get out. Just get someone here." David eyed the evidence and stepped to the hall.

Within seconds sirens wailed and David put his shoes back on and met with his personal guard outside the door. The relief guard had already arrived. "Sir?" the new man asked, saluting.

"Stay there. Someone has been inside my home."

The man went to call someone on his walkie-talkie. David stopped him. "DC police are on the way."

Several SWAT type patrol personnel carriers arrived in minutes and an armed troop raced out. David stopped them and said, "Inside my bedroom, near the left side by the dresser. Someone has tampered with the air duct."

"Have you cleared the home, sir?"

"No."

They nodded, got into attack formation, and entered.

David stood by as more patrol cars arrived. He never intended this to be a fiasco, but someone coming into his home without his knowledge and opening an air duct?

Not good.

A squad of uniformed DC police did a perimeter check of the residence. David had cameras in some locations, mainly aimed at the front and back door.

From inside he could hear the SWAT team yelling, '*Clear*!' as they went room to room.

A sergeant approached David. "No sign of forced entry, sir."
David nodded, waiting.

A dog was brought inside, sniffing the ground. David stepped back and wondered if he should call Deon, wondered if Deon was also under threat.

After a while, the man handling the dog returned and said, "It's not a bomb, sir. It's a camera."

"A camera."

"Yes, sir."

David entered his house with the police sergeant and walked to his room. The SWAT team had the vent open and David could see a small video camera had been placed inside.

"Hope it's not the NSA," the sergeant joked. When David did not smile, the man said, "Right. Do you want me to call the crime lab?"

"No. Just get rid of it."

The SWAT agent tore the camera out of the duct and screwed the plate back in place.

"Anything else?" David asked.

"No, sir. The dog went through the whole house and we checked all the other vents."

"Including the bathrooms?"

"Yes, sir. And light fixtures." He held up a device which detected electronic bugs.

"Thank you." David nodded. "That will be all."

The men began to leave his home and the sergeant asked David, "How would you like this handled?"

"No report. Nothing. Leave it to me."

"Yes, sir." He saluted David and everyone but his personal bodyguard left. David allowed the man to stand outside, at his post, then headed to his office.

He knelt in front of a cabinet and unlocked it, then rewound his surveillance video. No one approached the front or back door since he had left the house for the dinner. But, then, the screen went completely black for nearly twenty minutes, then returned with a fuzzy blink, and again, showed nothing. David rewound the video and again and could see twenty minutes of blank tape. So, not only was this person bold enough to stick a camera in his bedroom, he also gained access to a secure server, and deleted the electronic footage.

David relocked the cabinet and stood thinking for a minute, then he called Deon. It went to his voicemail. David knew Deon was getting ready for his show. "Deon, someone entered my home and planted a video camera in my bedroom. When you get back to your hotel, look at your room carefully. Tell you security guard to look." David checked the time and disconnected the call. He resumed changing his clothing and realized, if someone did not break in, then it had to be a person with a key.

And that was limited to two members of his staff and his immediate family.

David paused to think, and then called his ex-wife.

Chapter 10

Deon stood before a full length mirror as the madness of behind the scenes at the fashion show whirled around him. Clair was standing near a rack of clothing raising her voice as she spoke to someone in French, and then using a clipboard and pen, nodded as she was instructed on Deon's changes of clothing and timing of his appearances.

Deon was only wearing briefs and made sure his cock and balls appeared sensual in the small attire. An assistant used cream and then powder on his skin to make him gleam in the spotlights, and a woman stood behind him brushing his hair and spraying it with a light sheen.

Clair stood beside Deon and pointed to her board as she spoke in French, "Briefs by Calvin Klein, then casual style, slacks and shirt; Christian Dior, new fall wardrobe suit and jacket and tie; Ralph Lauren."

"Isn't it unusual to start with the briefs?" Deon didn't move as his assistants finished preparing him.

"Some yes, some no." Clair shrugged. "Hurry, time to line up."

Deon got the nod from his two stylists and walked to stand in a forming line of models that were getting ready to show off the famous new designs.

Hands surrounded him from behind, and Deon glanced back to see a fellow model he had a casual affair with several months ago. "Joaquin Griffin...you get me hard and I shall slap you," he said in French.

"Deon, Deon..." Joaquin inhaled him and went for a lick of Deon's neck. "Why do you never return my calls?"

Deon felt Joaquin urge him against his body, they were both only in briefs.

"I could fuck you here." Joaquin pushed his cock into Deon's ass. "You smell edible."

"*Dangereux...*" Deon laughed as they inched forwards as the music began and announcements of the fashion designers were heard over a loud speaker.

"Mm...Mark Antonious. Did you get to see him?"

"Indeed. How can I not see the legend?" Deon felt Joaquin trying to slide his fingers into the front of his briefs. "Stop it." He swatted Joaquin's hand.

"After the show? Hmm? You and me?" Joaquin began kissing the back of Deon's neck, caressing his arms from his elbows to his shoulders.

Deon shrugged him off. "I am seeing someone."

"Who?" Joaquin continued to caress Deon's arms lightly from behind. "And so what? Are you already committed to him?"

Deon again brushed Joaquin's hand off his arms. "No commitment yet, but still."

Clair appeared, looking rushed and when she noticed Joaquin behind Deon, she said, "Do not distract him. Look at what he is wearing. You make him erect I will slap you."

Deon laughed. "Don't worry. He won't."

"No?" Joaquin sounded shocked.

Deon turned to look over his shoulder at the handsome model. "No. I still have the taste of my lover's cum in my mouth."

Clair threw up her hands in disbelief and walked off with her clipboard.

"Who is this lover?" Joaquin made sure his cock kept rubbing Deon's ass every time they moved forward.

Again Deon swatted at Joaquin. "Stop. You're distracting me."

"Good." Joaquin kissed Deon's neck. "Does he have a name?"

"It's not your business."

"Is he a model?"

"No. Stop. We are too close to the runway." Deon nudged Joaquin back.

A man waved Deon closer to the stage and held him still as the designer underwear was being modeled first and men and women walked to the end of the catwalk and back while loud music played and lights flashed.

"Go." The man nodded and signaled to Deon.

He threw back his head proudly and began to walk in the spotlight, feeling strong, indeed like a lion that had a fierce powerful lover. He walked by a female model in a bra and matching panties and made his debut at the front of the stage, standing still as cameras flashed. He looked for David but it was too difficult to see in the crowd. Deon turned on his bare feet and headed back as Joaquin made his move to walk by him. Joaquin gave Deon a sexy smile, and Deon just met his gaze and didn't return it. The moment he was behind the curtain, he was grabbed and taken to the rack for his next wardrobe change.

Deon looked up and noticed his security guard nearby.

Clair asked Deon, "Do you want me to have him keep Joaquin away?"

"He is harmless." Deon put a pair of silky slacks on and Clair helped him with the shirt.

Joaquin grabbed Deon's ass as he hurried by to his own wardrobe change.

Deon jumped at the act, and Clair shook her head. "You gay men drive me crazy."

"Don't blame me." Deon felt someone brushing his hair and tried to find a mirror but was not standing near one. "Is David here?"

"I have not had time to look." Clair told Deon, "Tuck in the shirt, here is your belt."

"Where is my phone?"

"I have all your things safely stored. Not now. You have to focus."

"What if something happened to him?" Deon tucked in his shirt and stepped into leather loafers as a man crouched down for him, holding them.

"Deon Gael!" Clair yelled in exasperation, "He is the senator! It is not your job to protect him."

Deon heard from across the dressing area, "A senator?" from Joaquin.

Deon grew annoyed at Clair and Joaquin, but said, "Why is there no mirror?"

"Here." Clair dragged Deon by his arm to a full length mirror. Deon gave himself a quick look front and back.

"Hurry! Hurry!" the director of the event clapped and waved them over.

They were once again placed in a line formation and Joaquin, behind him whispered, "A handsome man of power?"

"Yes."

"Are you in love?"

"I just met him." Deon ran his hand over his hair.

"Is he here?"

"I assume so."

"You must introduce me. Does the public know he is gay?"

"Yes." Deon became exasperated. "Can we play twenty questions later?"

"I would love to play later." Joaquin went for Deon again, trying to spoon him.

Deon grew upset and pushed Joaquin away. "Why must you exasperate me?"

"You didn't say that when you had your beautiful cock in my ass."

Clair shot Joaquin a look that could kill, but Deon knew Joaquin was conceited enough not to care.

They were waved to go on. Deon inhaled, straightened his posture, and began his walk down the narrow aisle, passing the same woman who was wearing a colorful flowing outfit. Suddenly Deon spotted David. He didn't know if he had just arrived or Deon simply had not seen him before. Beside David was his security guard and David was one row from the front, but clearly able to see the show.

Deon made eye contact with David when he came to the end of the stage, and David met his gaze but appeared preoccupied. He did not smile.

Deon spun around and walked off, walking by Joaquin and avoiding his gaze.

Immediately Deon was rushed for his next clothing change and quickly stepped out of his outfit as the suit and tie were held up for him.

"He is here, Clair." Deon put the slacks of the suit on. "But he appears upset. Something has happened."

"Please…think about it later." She looped the neck tie around her own neck and began knotting it. Again Deon slipped on a different pair of shoes and Clair took off the tie and carefully placed it around Deon's collar and he drew up the knot as someone folded his collar from behind and helped him with the suit jacket. A small folded scarf was placed in the suit jacket pocket and Deon buttoned one button of the jacket, made sure the belt buckle was in the correct spot on his pants and rushed back to the lineup.

~

David held a program in his hand but wasn't interested in it. He glanced at the security guard who insisted on being beside David, since the unauthorized entry into his home. David had not been able to contact Deon and now, of course, he could see why. How the models were able to change and get back out to the catwalk so quickly amazed him.

Applause rang out as each model showed off the new French designs and both the men and women appeared perfect, flawless, like living mannequins; tall, thin, and painted.

David grew bored and lost in his head until Deon appeared. His lover moved with grace and elegance, meeting David's eye again as he wore a spectacular outfit; a dark shimmering suit, jacket and tie, and if David were not so preoccupied he would have returned the look of hungry lust in Deon's gaze.

After unbuttoning the jacket, Deon spun on his leather heels and walked back behind the curtain as another handsome male model scanned the crowd, met David's gaze, looked at the uniformed man beside him, and smirked.

Trying to read that expression, David sat up and studied the man as, he too, walked behind a curtain and a few women lingered to show their outfits.

Then, all of the models exited the curtain, lined the catwalk and stood still as the crowd rose to their feet and applauded. David stood, set his program down and clapped, seeing Deon staring at him with an apprehensive expression, as if he could read David's preoccupation.

When the noise of clapping died down, David caught the other male model fondle Deon's bottom discreetly as they vanished behind the curtain.

David sat down as the rest of the group stood to chat excitedly with the designers and some left the room to attend cocktail parties or late dinners.

The guard took his seat beside David and scanned the crowd like a watchdog.

A few moments later, Deon appeared from the same spot where he walked out from behind the curtain and hurried towards him.

"David?"

"Did you get any of my messages?" David rose to his feet.

The other model made his way through the crowd and leaned against Deon from behind. The comfortable way in which this model touched 'his' man, made David wonder what was going on.

Deon elbowed Joaquin to get off of him and David's guard stepped closer as if to intervene.

The man said something to Deon in French.

Deon rolled his eyes and gestured to David. "Senator, this is Joaquin Griffin. He is also model."

"Yes. I saw him on the stage." David did not reach out his hand in greeting. "Getting acquainted with your ass."

Joaquin laughed loudly and Deon said, "We had brief affair, now he thinks he owns it." Deon gave Joaquin a look of annoyance. "You have met him. Goodbye."

Joaquin whispered to Deon in French and left.

David bristled, not liking the handsome young man touching Deon.

Deon stood before David and asked, "What has happened? You look as if something horrific has occurred."

"Do you want to spend time with that other model?" David pointed.

"No!" Deon made a face of disapproval. "He is finished. He is pest."

David turned to walk to the exit.

Deon called, "David!"

Trying to keep his thoughts from ruining his night, David stopped and turned around.

"Please." Deon pouted.

"Get over here."

Deon moved closer and David held him in his arms. In his ear, David said, "I am worried about you."

"You see me. I am fine." Deon rested his chin on David's shoulder and pressed his head against David's.

"Are you tired? Do you need to go back to your hotel?"

"I go back only to play with you." Deon pretended to straighten David's tie.

"I would love that." David looked around. "Where is your security guard?"

"He is in back. I can get him. He is with my belongings and Clair. Yes? I wanted to make sure you don't leave without me."

"I'll go with you." David held Deon's hand and the guard followed them to the area behind the curtain. David couldn't believe the chaos of models rushing around and throwing items of clothing at assistants as they raced to their next engagements.

David spotted Clair and the guard as Deon made his way to her, collecting his phone, wallet and other personal items.

An exchange was made in French between the two. Deon appeared surprised and smiled then took clothing from Clair which was hung in a garment bag.

Clair waved at David and left.

The guard took the bag from Deon and both men approached him.

"Something good happen?" David asked.

"I get gifted all clothing I wear. Is sometimes happen, sometimes not."

David touched the suit Deon wore. "It's fantastic. No one could wear it better."

"Can I kiss my lion?" Deon pressed his chest against David's.

David didn't hesitate. He cupped Deon's jaw and kissed him. "Can we go back to your hotel?" David whispered.

"Of course. Two cars. Shh. Discreet."

David caressed Deon lovingly and they left the backstage area together.

As they did, David caught the jealous gaze from Joaquin as the man changed outfits.

Was he the source of their problems? No. That man did not own a key to David's home. And the list of people who did was disturbing David.

After speaking to his ex-wife, he was even more concerned.

The men managed to exit the Convention Center through the crowd and David was escorted to his sedan by his security/driver while Deon went in the opposite direction with his.

David kept his eye on Deon for as long as he could and then sat in the backseat of the sedan feeling very tired. He had paperwork to read over for the coming week's hearings, speeches to review, and a debate approaching with his opposing candidates. There were four people with hopes of being selected as the next individual to run for office from his own party, and David had to brush up on where they each stood on the major issues, issues that influenced the American public the most; jobs, wars, economy, housing, and the environment.

Although David had a strong conservative stand on law enforcement and capital punishment, he was the most liberal of his peers. Overtly since he was gay, but he had backed change in drug laws, as well as the science behind global warming, women's rights, equal pay…all the issues that alienated his party from the far right.

He didn't think he would have any problems winning against the republican candidate. It was getting the nomination from within his own party that he worried about.

What was the country ready for? A woman? A gay man? Or were they headed back to a white slightly more conservative candidate? The polls swayed like the maple trees in the warm breeze.

David's phone buzzed and he was so worn out he wanted to ignore it. Instead he took a quick look.

His Press Secretary, Leona Whitman sent him a text. '*you're being smeared on twitter again.*'

David didn't care. He looked at the traffic they were mired in as they drove to Deon's hotel, and then finally asked his secretary, '*what now?*'

She sent him the tweet.

'*#Senatordillhole#whorewithaids#rejectAshersenator sleeping with whore with AIDS*' The moniker of the creep was '*weknowtruth*'.

David texted her. '*ignore*'.

'*yes, senator.*'

David put his phone into his pocket and stared out of the window, amazed at the anonymous bullying that had hit. He had been a target before, when he first came out, but now that he was seeing Deon? It felt as if he had angered someone...personally. And when he thought about the conversation he had with his ex-wife, it actually made him sick to his stomach.

Chapter 11

Deon's driver parked in front of the hotel lobby entrance. He looked behind him and did not see David's car but knew he was on his way in the heavy traffic which left from the Convention Center.

The driver came around to open the door for Deon, then popped the trunk and removed the garment bag.

A valet approached and asked, "May I park the car for you?"

The guard appeared slightly concerned.

Deon took the garment bag and told the guard, "Is okay to go park yourself. I will wait inside lobby for the senator."

"Are you sure?" the uniformed man asked.

"Yes. Is fine." Deon touched the man's arm.

He walked Deon to the lobby, took a look inside it and then nodded. "I'll be right back. If you're not here, I'll be standing outside your room."

"Of course. Thank you." Deon waited by the glass door as the guard returned to the car and moved it himself.

Deon wondered what type of world they lived in to have to be so afraid. It was terrible when he thought about it.

And why were he and David under attack?

Jealousy? Homophobia? Revenge? Or simply no reason at all.

Deon held the top of the hanger over his shoulder and leaned against the wall so he could see out of the glass windows and doors. Another sedan pulled up and Deon felt his stomach flip in excitement because he knew it was his lover.

The driver opened the door for David and it appeared a similar discussion was occurring. David looked at the hotel and pointed to Deon, then the driver nodded and drove the sedan himself to park, not allowing the valet access to the key either.

Deon smiled at David as he approached, but David seemed preoccupied and exhausted, and did not meet Deon's gaze until he was standing in front of him. "Let's go." David gestured to the lobby and elevator.

Deon walked quickly with David and they rode the elevator up to the third floor. As David waited, Deon removed his card key and fumbled with the garment bag.

David took the bag without a comment, and Deon opened the hotel door. David entered first and looked around. The maid service had come, so the room was neat, the bed made, and the towels fresh.

Deon closed and latched the door, then took the garment bag from David and brought it to the bedroom of the suite to hang in his closet. Once he did, he removed his shoes and asked, "Something is the matter. I know. What is it?"

David glanced around the living room of the suite. "This room have a wet bar?"

"Yes." Deon opened a cabinet which was filled with every type of booze one would crave.

While David poured vodka into a glass, Deon removed the expensive jacket of his suit and loosened his tie. As David appeared to need to unwind, Deon entered the bedroom suite and hung up his new designer clothing, stripping down to his briefs and stood in the bathroom to wash his face and hands.

He noticed he still had powder on his skin from the fashion show, so he took off the briefs and walked to the shower stall, turning on the water to warm it up.

His hand held under the spray until the water warmed, Deon entered the stall and closed his eyes as the water washed over him. He too, was exhausted and running on adrenalin and nerves.

Movement at the bathroom door caught his eye.

David entered the bathroom, slid back the sliding door and watched Deon shower. A glass was in David's hand and he wasn't smiling, yet certainly enjoyed watching Deon.

"Join?" Deon reached out his hand.

David finished the contents of his glass and left the bathroom. When he returned he was naked, and stepped into the shower.

Deon moved back, allowing David the showerhead and soaped up his hands, massaging David's shoulders and neck.

A low moan came from David and he braced himself on the tiled wall with his hands.

Deon continued to wash his back, down to his bottom, and then used his soapy hands between David's legs. David spread his stance and rested against the wall and allowed Deon to play.

Deon reached through David's thighs to his balls and tugged them gently, feeling David's cock grow as he fondled him with his slippery hands. Deon soaped up his own cock and used it to run up and down the length of David's ass crack.

David spun around and went for Deon's mouth.

The taste of the vodka on David's lips, Deon swooned at the masculine touch and was backed up against the far wall of the shower. David rinsed Deon's cock with the rushing water, then knelt down and took it into his mouth.

Deon closed his eyes and let out a low moan of pleasure. He held David's shoulders as David's head bobbed forward and back, sucking to the base of Deon's cock and David's finger pushing into Deon's ass. *I know who will be the lion tonight*.

Deon went limp against the tiled wall and watched this handsome man of power suck him until he came.

Deon grabbed David's wet hair and his body went tense at the rush and David moaned as he tasted Deon's cum and massaged him for more.

"David…" Deon knees became weak and for some reason he felt emotional, then suspected it was because he was so tired.

David released Deon's cock from his lips and asked, "Can I make love to you?"

"Of course, my lion." Deon drew David upward and kissed him, tasting himself on David's tongue, no longer the vodka.

After a passionate moment of kissing, Deon whispered, "You let me prepare. Yes?"

David embraced Deon, nearly picking him up off his feet. "Yes." He chewed on Deon's neck and earlobe and Deon felt his eyes burn with tears of love and joy.

David reached for the taps and turned them off, then stepped out and rubbed his hair and back with the towel.

Deon stood watching him in the steamy room, and rested against the wall of the shower, in love, whether he liked it or not. Madly, deeply, in love with a U.S. senator.

David glanced back as he tossed the towel over the rack. "I'll be waiting."

"Yes." Deon smiled but it felt as if he needed to shed tears.

David gave him a similar smile back and left the bathroom.

Deon took a fresh towel and wiped his eyes and face, trying to get his emotions under control.

~

David carried his glass to the wet bar and refilled it. He tossed the third shot of vodka down his throat and set the glass down, trying to stop thinking.

Too many thoughts were hitting him and all he wanted was to make love to Deon and get lost in the touch of a man.

On his way back to the bedroom, David stopped for a moment to look out of the peephole of the hotel room door. Both guards were there, chatting together quietly.

David kept walking and picked up his clothing which he had shed when he was invited to shower. He folded it and placed it on a chair, then turned down the bed and looked into a drawer of the nightstand to see if Deon kept the condoms or lubrication there, but all that was in it was a Bible.

144

David closed the drawer, dropped down on the luxurious bed and stared at the ceiling. When his phone hummed he said, "Leave me alone. For crying out loud." He ignored it and heard the sink in the bathroom run, the toilet flush and then David stared at the enormous flat screen TV that was on the wall across from the foot of the bed.

The bathroom door opened and Deon set down condoms and lubrication on the nightstand, which he obviously had with his personal items in the bathroom. Deon lay beside David and kissed his nipple.

David touched Deon's damp hair and stared into his blue eyes.

"My lion." Deon caressed the hair on David's chest. "I must confess."

"What must you confess?" David cupped Deon's jaw affectionately.

"I love." Deon's eyes watered. "I know is soon."

David went for him, bringing Deon to lie on his body and embraced him. He closed his eyes and held him tight. "You make me so happy…so content." David kissed Deon's cheek and neck. "I don't know why we bonded so quickly."

Deon dabbed at the corner of his eye and leaned on his elbows so they could see each other. "Let me satisfy my lion."

"I am happy just to be here with you." David caressed Deon's cheek, seeing his eyes about to overflow.

"I want stay here. With you. Not leave."

David let out a long exhale. "I have been afraid to ask when you do have to leave."

"One more day." Deon wiped at his eyes again. "I feel like fool, yes? Lion is now not lamb, but child."

David cupped Deon's face and kissed him. When their lips met, Deon straddled David's hips and devoured him. A spark of lust made David's cock wake up from its soft state.

Deon whimpered and kissed his way down David's body.

The chills that rushed over David made him groan and spread his legs. Deon spent time kissing and sucking each of David's nipples, then chewed his way down David's treasure trail to his dick. He enveloped it and held it in his mouth, drawing patterns on it with his tongue while keeping it still.

David reached down for Deon and caressed him, beginning to crave a climax and take Deon, master him, dominate him.

As Deon's sucking and teasing gave David an erection, David glanced at the condoms and lubrication beside him. He reached to the nightstand and shut off a lamp that had been lit before he entered the room. He sat up, grabbed Deon and roughly pushed Deon face down on the bed.

Deon immediately surrendered control and positioned himself on his knees.

David inched his way behind this gorgeous model and admired him. With his thumb, he circled the tiny pink rim of Deon's perfectly groomed body and Deon let go a delicious moan of delight.

David kissed Deon's bottom and moved lower on the bed. With the fresh scent of soap and cologne on Deon's skin, David parted Deon's ass cheeks and did something he had never done before. He rimmed a man. Most of his gay porn had this act, and Deon had done it to him, but David had never done it to anyone. He had always imagined being slightly put off by the act, but Deon was so clean and obviously knew how to prepare, that David's timid little licks turned into a wild frenzy.

He darted his tongue into Deon's ass and Deon groaned loudly and arched his back.

David wiped his mouth and used his finger to massage that perfect puckered hole and then felt his cock throb, dying to get in. David went for the condom strip and Deon raised his bottom higher, eager as well.

David rolled on a condom, then used the lubrication on his finger and pushed inside Deon.

146

"David...*ohhh*..." and then French expletives followed that made David smile.

"Should I tie you up?" David pushed two fingers inside Deon.

"Tie me, gag me, I am yours to do as wish."

David's cock liked the sound of those words because it throbbed and swelled in anticipation. David slapped Deon's ass, simply because he had done it to him. Deon flinched and groaned, writhing on the bed.

The sense of power, having this man as his lover, was liberating to David. It was as if he was finally living his fantasies.

He couldn't wait or bother with binding Deon since he was so completely submissive without it. He knelt behind him, pointed his cock at Deon's ass, and slid in.

"Oh fuck!" David penetrated easily with the slick gel until he was balls deep. He kept still, feeling Deon squeeze his muscles around his cock to entice him. "Jesus..." David held onto Deon's hips and looked down at the contact, his cock burrowed into a man's ass. It was too good to be true. He began fucking him, thrusting slowly, since he was already on the edge. Deon clenched the bedding and David imagined him chewing on the pillow.

David rocked in and out of Deon and when Deon's body tensed up and he gasped, David had a feeling he had hit Deon's internal sweet spot, like Deon had done to him. "Does that feel nice?"

"David!" Deon crushed the pillows and pushed backwards to seal their bodies.

"Oh, Christ, Deon, I'm not going to last..." David tried to hold back.

"No. Go! Go..."

David held onto Deon and stared at his cock as it moved in and out of Deon's tight ass and the climax began to swirl through David's groin. He closed his eyes and pumped faster, harder.

Deon whimpered and David could feel his body pulsate with a climax from the inside of Deon's body. When he realized his lover was coming, David let go and hammered into Deon, the orgasm so intense he felt a sense of complete lightness and relief. He pushed as deeply as he could, then as the rush subsided, he slowly pulled out, staring at the amount of cum in the tip of the condom.

Deon touched himself and then rolled over, flushed and sweating.

David smiled. "I made you come."

"Oh *oui*! David! You love make so wonderful."

"Let me get rid of this." David stood off the bed and tugged at the condom, disposed of it and washed his hands and cock, then brought a soapy wet washcloth to his lover and gently cleaned him as well. Deon appeared sated, smiling and spent.

David returned to the bathroom and tossed the washcloth into the sink, then dropped onto the bed and held onto Deon, kissing him on the cheek as they both recuperated.

Phones buzzed from where they were on the dresser and in a trouser pocket.

"Can't they leave alone? Hmm?" Deon asked, "One night? Late? Both so tired. Why can they not stop call?"

"I don't know." David held onto Deon, closing his eyes. "They are a pain in the ass."

"We not robots. We need minute without call, call, call."

"We do." David kissed Deon's shoulder and rested his thigh over Deon's soft cock.

"I no even look anymore." Deon nestled against David.

"I don't want to. It's always bad news."

"I was glad you show up at fashion show because Clair took my phone. She was like angry mother...she say, no, no, no."

David smiled and felt as if he were going to fall asleep. Then he opened his eyes. "When did you give her your phone?"

"Uh...after dinner at hotel."

David sat up in the bed, startling Deon.

"What?" Deon held his chest.

"You...you didn't get any of my messages?"

"Which? Which messages?"

"I wanted your room swept clean of electronic bugs."

"Bugs?" Deon sat up. "Bugs?"

"Not like insects." David looked around the room. "Did your security guard get someone to inspect this room?"

"No. No one tell, but that may not mean it was not done."

"Shit." David hopped out of bed and slipped his briefs and pants on. "Cover up."

Deon brought the blanket higher on his naked body.

David turned on a bright overhead light and began inspecting the room.

"What do you look for? David?"

David scanned the room for the air duct. It was above the flat screen TV on the wall. A prime viewing spot for the bed. He walked closer and looked at the top of the television. White flakes were on it. "No. No way." David touched the dust and it was paint flakes. He grabbed the chair, dumping the rest of his clothing that was folded on it, and stood high, inspecting the vent. The paint from the screws had been disturbed.

A cold wash of chills hit David and he felt sick. "I need a screwdriver."

"I no have. I call for service?" Deon went to get out of the bed.

He hopped off the chair. "No. Hang on." David threw him a pair of trousers and briefs and said, "Stay there." He jogged to the hotel door and when it opened both guards jumped at the start. "I need one of you to go to the hotel desk and get a screw driver." He pointed to Deon's guard. "You."

"Yes, sir." He hurried off.

David brought his guard inside. He asked him quietly, "Was Deon's room checked for electronic devices?"

"I don't know. I didn't do it myself. Was his security supposed to?"

"I found a camera in my room. I thought someone was instructed to come here. Can you find out if they did?"

"Yes, sir." The young man took out his cell phone.

David began to scan the rest of the hotel room. Nothing was in the living or kitchen area. When he returned to the bedroom, Deon was dressed and appeared to be a nervous wreck. David bypassed him to the bathroom and held his breath as he pulled back the shower door. He spotted a tiny black transmitter attached to the showerhead. David ripped it off and stared at it in horror.

"Sir?"

David turned to Deon's security guard, who was out of breath and holding a screwdriver.

David handed him the camera he had found, climbed the chair and unscrewed the vent. Inside it was another recording device. David yanked it out and closed his eyes in disbelief.

~

Deon was terrified. He had no idea what was happening.

David's security guard was on the phone, then rushed to David and said, "Sir. A team was never dispatched. No one gave an order, or if they did, it was not followed."

David held out the tiny camera.

The man went pale. "Sir…what do you want me to do?"

"What is it? David!" Deon became frantic. "Is this same camera in last hotel shower?"

"Yes." David found his phone and put it to his ear, leaving the bedroom.

The two guards kept searching for something. More devices?

Deon felt dizzy and sat on the bed. *Why? Who cares this much to do this to us?*

He covered his face and tried to calm down, but his heart was racing.

Chapter 12

"Jim?" David said over his phone.

"What?"

"We need to talk."

"Do you know what time it is?"

David tried not to scream at his son. "I do. And I know you weren't sleeping."

"Yeah? How do you know that?"

"Because you've been a very busy boy, haven't you?"

"Why the hell do you care?"

"Where are you staying? Your mother said you don't even see her anymore." David glanced at the two guards who appeared to be searching for more secret cameras, but David figured, the bedroom and the shower. What other place could there be for the best footage, but he left them to feel useful.

"Fuck you."

"Jim…I know it was you."

"You don't know shit!"

"Why? Just tell me why?" David moved to a chair near the window of the hotel suite's living room and sat down. "What did I do to you to deserve this?"

Silence hit the other end of the phone, and David wondered if his son had hung up. Then he heard a slight breath. "Please. What did I do?" David asked again.

"Suddenly you're playing the concerned father?"

David felt sick and even though he and his ex-wife had some sense Jim was not himself lately, David wouldn't expect this type of behavior from his own flesh and blood. "I have never stopped being concerned for you or Veronica."

"Yeah? Do you even know what you put me through?"

David tried to think. "No. Obviously I don't. Why don't you fill me in?"

"You came out! You divorced mom and came out as a fag! I never heard the end of it. From the minute you did that to me, I have been teased constantly. You fucking idiot! You thought only of yourself!"

"Did you tell me or your mother you were being bullied?"

The guards seemed to give up on their hunt. David waved them out of the room. They left, back to their post.

"Fuck. You!"

"Jim, can't we have a conversation? You're nineteen, not five. I came out and divorced your mother two years ago."

"Yeah, but you didn't start flaunting it until this French fucking whore!"

David flinched and tried to keep his temper.

"I sucked his dick and fucked him, Dad! He's a slut!"

"Why would my straight son suck a man's dick or make love to another man?"

Jim grew silent.

"Jim?"

"I did it because I could. I'm not gay. I'm not a fag like you are."

"Because you could." David was completely confused and had a feeling so was his son.

"To prove to everyone you're a prick! To show the fucking planet what a self-centered asshole you are! So, now I can tell everyone that Senator Asher fucked and sucked the same man as his kid did."

David died inside. He had no idea he had led his son to this type of betrayal and neither did his mother. Jim could certainly ruin his chances at the White House with that story.

"So, you want to see me humiliated? My chance at election ruined?"

"Yes! Christ, are you stupid? Your fucking home office has so many goddamn degrees on the wall. You flaunt your education, your military record at everyone!"

"I didn't realize I did. I'm sorry if you feel this way." David was shocked. He caught something out of the corner of his eye and spotted Deon, looking worried, standing at the bedroom doorway.

"You're not sorry. You're full of shit. Ever since you moved out, you stopped caring about me."

"I have never stopped caring about you or your sister. Or your mother. I have no idea why you think that."

"When was the last time I saw you?"

"I'm busy, but during the breaks, Veronica seems to be able to stop by. She was over my place earlier today."

Jim snickered. "Yeah, so was I."

Rage grew in David and he bit it back, feeling as if his son now held a lot of power. If video proving both father and son fucked the same man? David was finished politically.

"What do you want me to do?" David asked softly.

"Dump him! He's a fucking slut! He let me suck him!"

"Deon was not seeing me at that time, and he was free to do as he liked. And the second time, in the bathroom, he did not do that act willingly."

"Oh, he liked it. If he tells you he didn't he's a bullshitter."

"Jim...I need to see you."

"Why? You think seeing me will stop me from uploading the crap I just taped? You licking that slut's ass?"

David went cold and walked to the door, gesturing to his security guard for a pen and pad.

The man immediately took a pad from breast his pocket and handed David a pen. As David spoke he wrote, *'Trace this call, pick up my son, and place him in custody.'*

The guard read the note, looked stunned, nodded and grabbed his phone, walking down the hall as he made the call.

David returned to the living room. Deon sat on the sofa nearby.

"So…" David stayed calm and tried to keep his son on the line. "My being out was bad enough, and now that I am dating someone, it's over the top? Am I right?"

"Yes! I had to stop seeing the guys I used to hang out with. The jocks and cool guys. They fucking teased the shit out of me. They said, you're dad's gay, you must be."

David thought that may be exactly correct, but Jim was under pressure at the moment to fit into college. "So, instead of telling them to stop bullying you, or talking to me or your mother—"

"You see? You don't get it! Oh, sure, Dad, tell them to stop bullying me, please. Yeah, that works. You moron. You are so out of it. You have no idea what they did to me."

"Is it like what you did to Deon? What you are doing to me?"

"No! You deserve it. I didn't do anything!"

"I deserve it. Deon deserves it." David met Deon's look of intense concern. "Why?"

"You flaunted it! It was bad enough to just know you were a fag! But to be seen with a guy? Some French asshole because he's so good looking?"

"I am not dating Deon just because he is handsome."

"Sure, Dad. Keep telling yourself that. And he's like twenty-fucking-nine! You make me sick."

"Okay. So, in your reality of how I should be, I am to never be happy, never have a partner…"

"Yes! You don't deserve it. You left us. You left me, mom, and Veronica!"

"But, they seem okay. They have never been cruel to me. Never told me the things you're telling me."

"Fuck them."

"And the new friends you're hanging around with? Pretty good with computers and gadgets?"

"Yeah, sucks to be you."

David could not believe the hostility from his own son. He felt as if he had been blind to see this coming. And he really was shocked. He knew Lydia would be stunned to find out her own son perpetrated these miserable acts against him.

"If you could have your way, what punishment would you like to see happen to me?" David checked his watch and wondered how long it would take to track this call and get his son.

"Well, I want you to lose the bid for president, you don't deserve that. You suck."

"Okay. What else?"

"Be locked up in jail? Gang raped or something? Taught a lesson."

David cringed and rubbed his face. "You want me in jail and gang raped."

Deon covered his mouth in shock.

"Payback's a bitch."

David asked, "Payback for being the reason you were bullied."

"Yup. Those degrees finally kicking in, Dad?"

"So, in order for you to stop this smear campaign against me, you want to see me ruined, violated and incarcerated. Is that truly how you feel? You have nothing left for me? No affection? No love?"

"Shut up."

David heard Jim's voice crack. "And I was a terrible Dad to you growing up, right? Never took you to a ballgame, never threw Frisbees with you in the park, never went to see action movies…"

"Shut up! You think the shit you did when I was ten makes up for this now?"

"I guess it doesn't. I guess nothing I can do will make it up to you. So you and me? Lost? Gone?"

He heard a sob break from his son and felt ill. "Jimmy...where are you?"

"At a friend's house. Away from you."

"I know seeing me date is hard. Believe me."

"You don't know shit!"

David backed off. "I don't, you're right." He heard a door crash open over the phone. Shouts from police ordering his son to get on the floor.

David felt so miserable he covered his eyes as he listened.

The phone was dropped and it sounded as if either DC SWAT or the Secret Service had taken over the residence. The phone was picked up and someone said, "Hello?"

"This is Senator David Asher. Is my son in custody?"

"Yes, sir. Where would you like him taken?"

"My ex-wife's home, please. And tell him I will be there shortly."

"Yes, sir."

David hung up and Deon was staring at him. "It was my son."

Deon covered his mouth and appeared devastated.

David called his ex-wife.

"David? What's wrong?"

"Sorry to wake you. Jim was the one posting the smear campaign on the 'net. He's in custody and I am having him brought to you."

"Oh, my God? Jimmy did this to you?"

"Yes. I'm sorry, Lydia. Can I meet you there? I don't want to put him into a holding cell."

"Oh, my God."

"I know. Believe me. I'm as sick as you are. See you soon." He disconnected the line and couldn't believe anything he had just learned.

"No," Deon said, shaking his head. "Say is not son! Say I not touch son!"

David stood up and walked to the bedroom to finish getting dressed.

~

Deon felt like gagging. How could a son do this to his father? And now? Now that David knew his son had sucked him? Fucked him? Deon had no doubt he must truly seem like a slut to David.

He had no idea what to do.

David appeared from the bedroom, looking so hurt Deon was in agony.

Deon stood slowly, meeting him at the door. "So? *Fini*? This is you and my goodbye?"

"I can't think straight right now." David rubbed his forehead. "I'm going to talk to him with his mother. I just hope he hasn't downloaded you and me making love just now. Because if he has, I'm ruined."

"David." Deon felt like throwing up. "Blame me. Is me. No take blame."

"I'll call you." David touched Deon's cheek and walked out of the hotel room.

"David…" Deon watched David leave with his security guard. "David!" He began crying.

David didn't turn around and left his sight.

Deon's guard asked, "Can I get you anything?"

Shaking his head, Deon wiped at his eyes. "Nothing you can buy for broken heart." He closed the door, fell on the bed face down and wept.

~

As his driver took him to his wife's home, outside the city center core of DC to a suburb away from the crime and chaos, David read his watch. It was nearing one in the morning. He finally checked the missed calls, and as he suspected, they were from his staff.

David put the phone to his ear and called Eric.

Sounding as if he woke him, Eric answered the phone. "David."

"It was Jimmy, Eric."

"What?"

"Jimmy." David stared out of the window, but not really looking at anything. "He was the one who made this whole smear campaign, used a key to get into my home, and also planted cameras in both of Deon's hotel rooms. So he now has footage of me and Deon making love and showering together."

"How on earth did you figure out it was him?"

"Lydia and I had a chat earlier this evening. She said he's been hanging around with a new group of kids that she did not like, and he does not come home at all anymore. She didn't even know where he was staying."

"Good Lord."

"So, after Deon and I made love, I noticed the same thing I did at my house. The vent, the showerhead, both had cameras. Sadly, too late."

"I was trying to call you, to tell you more terrible things were being sent over the tweeters."

David tried not to correct Eric, since his generation was so new to the social networks. "I know. Leona texted me as well."

"Jimmy? How can that be? He's such a sweet boy."

"He's nineteen and not so sweet anymore. I had his number traced and the SWAT team made entry and took him into custody. I'm meeting them with him, and Lydia, at Lydia's house to talk to him."

"What can I do, David?"

"Well, Eric…if word gets out that Deon screwed both father and son? I think that's the end of my campaign bid."

"Oh, dear Lord.

"You think you're ill over it?" David made a noise in his throat. "I'm sick to my stomach."

"I don't know what to say."

"Nothing you can say, Eric. But at least we finally know who it is."

"Jimmy? How can it be Jimmy? Oh, your father would be so angry."

"Ya know…you're right, Eric. I know it's late, but, can you come to Lydia's house? You are like a grandfather to him. Maybe since Dad can't be there…"

"I'm on my way."

"Thanks, Eric."

David disconnected the line and stared out of the window. He thought about Deon allowing his nineteen year old son to suck his dick. No, the restaurant was not voluntary, but… the blowjob? That was.

Was Deon a slut?

David rubbed at his eyes and leaned his arm on the door of the car, so tired, he could not think straight.

But he had a lot to deal with now. And somehow he had to decide with his ex-wife, the proper punishment for his son.

Prison and gang-raped. David shook his head sadly. He had no idea he had hurt his son so much that he could say something like that to him. David choked up with emotion and then swallowed it back and gained control.

He went wrong. Somewhere during the divorce, coming out, and trying to be strong and powerful, showing the world being a gay man did not mean he was weak, he had somehow harmed his son. And he simply did not know if the damage done was too much, and there was nothing he could do to repair it.

G. A. HAUSER

Chapter 13

When David arrived at his wife's home he was upset to see not only police vehicles but the media.

"Fuck!" David leaned closer to his driver and said, "How the hell did they get wind of this?"

"They are scavengers, Senator. They can smell a fresh scandal scent for miles."

"Pull up as close as you can." David pointed to Lydia's private home.

Police were actually keeping back the press and it was growing into a huge mess that he knew was going to end his campaign hopes.

The guard opened David's door and blocked him from the cameras as he and David headed to the house. David was allowed in by a uniformed officer, and when he stepped inside, his wife, his daughter, and his son, were in the living room, along with the DC police officers that had brought him in. Jim was in flex cuffs, tied in front, and David could not believe how Jim looked. It certainly had been a long time, since his own son appeared to be a stranger to him.

He had a pierced lip and eyebrow, and his badly chewed fingernails were painted black. He wore a black T-shirt with a red 'Anarchist' symbol on it, baggy low shorts that hung past his knees, and high-top tennis shoes without laces. In other words, he looked like a street punk. And…he had shaved his head.

Everyone shut up when David entered.

Lydia appeared beside herself with grief and his daughter leaned against the wall near the hallway, looking at her brother with complete disgust.

More noise was heard at the door and Eric Sutten entered, appearing rushed and in a pair of slacks and dress shirt, with a sweater-vest over it, holding his walking stick. The minute he laid eyes on Jimmy he appeared as stunned as David was.

David gestured for the police to leave the house.

The sergeant nodded and waved to the one other officer in the room to leave. David asked the sergeant before he left, "Does he need to be cuffed like that?"

"He assaulted the officers."

"Any injuries?"

"No, Senator. But we didn't want him to harm your ex-wife or daughter."

David looked at his son who would not meet his eyes. "Take them off."

The sergeant nodded and his officer removed a Leatherman's tool and snipped the plastic cuffs off. Then, with the sergeant, the police officer left so they could talk as a family.

Eric said to David, "I have Leona coming to deal with the press."

"Good." David moved closer to his son.

He got a sneer as if his son was going to get up and hit him.

Veronica said, "Aren't you at least going to apologize to Dad?"

"For what?" Jimmy showed his teeth as he snarled.

Lydia asked in shock, "For what?"

Eric shook his head. "Your grandfather would be so ashamed of you."

"Of me?" Jimmy rubbed his sore wrists. "I'm not a fag fucking a slut!"

"You need to get a life!" Veronica yelled at him.

"Fuck you! You've always been his favorite!"

David was so shocked by the appearance of his son, he simply didn't know how to handle this.

Lydia, her arms folded over her knitted pink shawl, asked, "Why do you think we favored your sister? You had everything she had."

Veronica said, "Yeah, and so what if Dad dates? Jesus, Jimmy, grow the fuck up!"

David held his hand up to Veronica. "Okay. Calm down." David asked, "Can I speak to my son in private?"

Veronica snorted and said, "Good luck," and left the room.

Lydia gave David a sweet caress on his cheek and followed her daughter out, into the kitchen.

David noticed Eric lingering. "I'll let you know if I need you."

Eric nodded, patted David's back and followed the women out.

David walked a little closer to his son and then crouched down in front of him. "I'm sorry."

Jim rolled his eyes and crossed his arms over his chest.

"I'm sorry for not knowing. I'm sorry for ever hurting you. For whatever role my coming out played in you getting bullied. I'm sorry."

Jim quickly brushed at his eyes and then didn't answer.

David moved to sit near him, slowly, to make sure Jim didn't object. Jim stayed still and rubbed at the slight redness to his wrists from where he was cuffed.

David sighed and leaned his elbows on his knees. "I knew when I left your mom and came out there would be fallout. But I never guessed it would hit you."

Jim didn't answer, but didn't say anything nasty for once.

As he thought about the situation, David rubbed the new coarse growth on his jaw. "I tried to pretend it wasn't selfish. I stayed true to your mom the entire time we were together. Never strayed. Not once." David could hear his son's breathing beside him but didn't look at him.

"I don't know why I got married. I have been gay my whole life. But…your grandfather told me if I had any type of political aspirations I had to hide." David remembered the day he told his father he was gay. He was eighteen.

"I thought long and hard about that. At first I was angry. I thought why should I have to hide who I am?" David felt Jim shift on the sofa but he didn't react. "All through my military service, I had to deal with Don't Ask Don't Tell.

"I met your mom in grad school and I did love her. She was kind, giving…and she knew."

Jim spun his head around quickly and David felt his gaze on his profile.

"She knew. She knew I was gay. She knew I needed her to make it in politics and of course, we slept together, or you and Veronica would not be here."

David didn't look at his son. He wasn't sure he could stand the hatred he figured would be in his eyes.

Taking a breath first, David continued, "We stayed together until you and Veronica were old enough to deal with our divorce, my coming out…or at least your mother and I thought so. Of course Veronica is a little older, and maybe it's different for girls."

Jim swallowed loudly but David still did not have the courage to look at him.

"So…" David stared across the room, at family photos, could hear the murmuring of the other three in the kitchen, and it sounded as if Lydia had turned on a coffee pot. "I divorced your mom, announced I was gay…at a time in politics where I could sense the opening of a door. I knew once all fifty states had cleared the way for gay marriage, my life wouldn't be scrutinized as terribly as perhaps it would have been five years ago."

Jim chewed on a fingernail. David could see it out of the corner of his eye.

"But I didn't date. Not once. I figured knowing I was gay and the public actually seeing me with a man…"

Jim cleared his throat and shifted on the sofa.

David waited to see if he wanted to say anything but his son didn't. So David continued, "…I…I weakened. I was lonely. I'm only human, Jimmy. I guess I needed love, affection…"

Jim covered his face with his hands and leaned his elbows on his knees.

David looked over at him, still trying to get over the difference in Jim's appearance from the family photos on the bureau and the shaven-headed, bloated kid beside him with the piercing and odd clothing.

"It wasn't love at first sight with Deon. He seemed nice." David shrugged. "I never expected to meet someone to date at the fundraiser. And with the debates coming up, I figured I'd just lay low, as I had been. The celibate fag candidate."

David felt Jim look at him.

This time David braved a glance back. They met eyes. Hatred did not burn in Jim. But David struggled to see the young man he had once loved and had a great relationship with.

David shrugged. "And now? I have a son who wants me gang-raped and in jail for my crime. But I still don't know what the crime is. Shouldn't my son be angry at the intolerant idiots who teased him? Why me?"

Jim rubbed at his eyes again, still silent.

"And the smear campaign you hit me with? The videos, the stalking of Deon? I wish you were in the Secret Service, because you did one hell of a job killing my career and keeping anonymous."

A sob came from Jim and the relief David felt was enormous. He took a chance and put his arm around him.

Jim leaned on David and cried.

"Okay, baby." David rubbed his back. "It's okay."

David let him cry and held him, struggling with the pain he had caused his son unknowingly.

~

Deon couldn't sleep. He paced, felt caged, and had no idea what to do. It was very late. He opened his hotel door and his security guard stood up, from leaning against the wall.

"Is bar in hotel, yes?"

"I don't know." The man rubbed his eyes. "I can find out."

"I no can rest. I no can stay here."

The guard waited for instructions.

"You know of bar?"

"I'm sure the front desk may have a suggestion."

"Good." Deon made sure he had his wallet and phone and left the room. The two men walked to the elevator. Deon checked his phone, dying to ask David how he was. But how would he be feeling after knowing his lover had sex with his son and his son was responsible for terrible things?

They exited the elevator at the lobby floor, and both the guard and Deon headed to a clerk manning the desk.

The guard asked, "Do you know of a decent nightclub nearby?"

"There's one right around the corner. Just one block to the right." He pointed.

"Thanks." The guard tilted his head and he walked with Deon outside. The air had cooled and humidity had lessened.

Within a few minutes a tavern, filled with people, was visible. The guard said, "I can't go inside with a gun. I'll be right here."

"Yes, well...since David find person...go. No need."

"Are you sure?"

"Yes. Threat is no more. You take good care of me." Deon took out his wallet to give the man cash.

The man held up his hand, refusing it. "No way. We can't accept tips. Okay. I'll head home. But call 911 if something happens."

Deon shook the man's hand. "You have been helpful. Yes?"

"Take care." The man waved and walked towards the hotel.

Deon entered the tavern and looked around. All the tables were occupied so he sat at the bar on an open seat between two men. Deon waited, seeing the bartender was very busy, so while he did, Deon scrolled through his messages and contacts. Finding one; he thought about it, and then texted. '*Are you awake?*'

'*yes*', immediately was typed back.

'*can come to Lima Lounge?*'

'*yes. as soon as I can.*'

Deon put his phone into his pocket and finally got the bartender's attention. "What cocktail is special here?" Deon asked.

"Lima Breeze?"

"Yes."

"We close at two, just so you know."

"Is fine." Deon checked the time on his phone, it was just after one. He noticed a few earlier text messages from Clair about more terrible tweets coming from the social network. He did not read them now that he was aware who had done it.

Fifteen minutes later, Deon felt a tap on his shoulder. He turned to see Joaquin.

Deon looked for another seat at the bar. But before he found one, Joaquin asked the couple sitting beside Deon if they would mind moving one seat down, allowing him and Deon to sit together. They shifted over kindly, and Joaquin sat beside Deon, looking at him.

Deon gave Joaquin a look he knew betrayed his anguish.

In French, Joaquin asked Deon, "How many have you had?" pointing to the cocktail glass.

166

Deon held up three fingers.

Joaquin nodded.

The bartender placed a coaster down in front of Joaquin and asked him, "What can I get you?"

"What he is having, and another for him."

"We close at two…"

"Yes. Is fine." Joaquin looked at Deon, full of concern. "This senator? Did he dump you?"

Deon covered his face and then in French so no one could understand them, he said, "David's son perpetrated a smear campaign against him. And used me to do it."

"How?"

"Before David and I were together this young man came to my room in the previous hotel." Deon stopped talking as the bartender brought out two more drinks.

"Thank you." Joaquin nodded and sipped the drink. "Nice."

"I am very drunk. No food," Deon said.

"Continue." Joaquin sipped the drink.

"Well, the young man was not bad to look at, and offered to give me a blowjob." Deon shrugged. "I had not had sex for some time, so I allowed him to do it."

Joaquin nodded.

"He was posing as a hotel employee. I had no idea of course who he was, and well, I have had anonymous sex before."

"Who hasn't?"

"This young man, he begins to follow me, and finds David and I dining at a restaurant on Friday evening. He and another male trapped me in the men's room while David was unaware and he forced himself on me, with threats that if I did not comply he would harm David."

"No!" Joaquin held the drink away from his lips. "His son?"

"Yes." Deon gulped the strong cocktail, feeling very drunk.

"And now?"

"And now, David somehow has figured it out. He has had his son taken into custody. And he went to his ex-wife's home to meet and decide what to do with him." Deon glanced around but no one was listening, and he was certain they could not speak the language.

"So you have had sex with father and son?"

"Unwittingly. And with David attempting to run for president, I feel he has lost his chance if this information goes public."

"I heard rumors you were being slandered in the newspaper. I saw a retraction."

"Did you?" Deon hadn't heard about it since he spoke to the lawyer.

"You know, third page, two lines." Joaquin made a face of annoyance and waved his hand. "They were so sorry for the mistake and slander. But who will read that? All they read is the front page and the ruin of your reputation. Calling you a paid whore? I was disgusted and wondered what is wrong with this country."

Deon finished the drink quickly and set the glass down. "Now, I am sure I have lost him."

"How could it work? You are in Paris most of the time, and the rest of the time traveling to do the shows. You, like me, we can't have a real romance, no relationships, just sex in the night."

"I know that's the reality. I know." Deon felt his eyes burn.

Someone shouted out, "Last call!"

Deon knew what that meant. "One more."

Joaquin signaled the bartender for a refill for them both. He was acknowledged.

"Deon." Joaquin touched his back gently. "I teased you at the fashion show, but I do feel for you. I would love to settle down, have roots, not travel. But we are still in our prime and can work. Once we leave the catwalk, what can we do for a living?"

"I don't know. Mark Anontious, he is in his early forties, yet perfect in every way. He has a fabulous career in *Dangereux* as well as the upscale car manufacturer. He does not travel much, I would imagine, is married, has a son..."

"So, you would try to get a sponsorship? Do ads?"

Deon sat up as two new cocktails were placed before them, with a bill.

When Joaquin read the cost of the drinks he choked in amazement. "Sixty U.S. dollars?"

"Is nothing." Deon tossed a credit card at him. "Yes. I am going to try and see if Clair can find me a local modeling agent. Someone here."

"Here." Joaquin pointed down, as if indicating DC. He placed Deon's credit card with the tab. "No way. You have to be in New York or Los Angeles."

"You don't know that. Why not here?"

"This is the town of politics, not fashion and agents."

The bartender picked up their credit card and bill and walked away.

Deon and Joaquin downed the drinks like water.

When the bartender returned the credit slip, Deon wrote in a tip, and took his credit card back.

When he tried to stand up, he swayed and grabbed the bar stool.

"Oh no." Joaquin held him from falling. "You really did it. Now I have to carry you?"

Deon shook his head. "No. Just let me try to walk." Deon could barely move. "Yes. You have to help me." He hooked Joaquin by his elbow and leaned on him.

"I can't believe you have allowed this politician to steal your heart." Joaquin led Deon outside and they stopped. "Where are you staying?"

"Close. Just down the street." Deon kept a grip on Joaquin's arm.

"I'm glad. I heard at night it's not so safe to walk the streets."

"I heard that too." Deon looked up at the sign for his hotel.

"Oh. I suppose I need to call a taxi?" Joaquin asked, "Because you will not allow me to come to your room?"

"Come. Not for sex." Deon wagged his finger and could barely see he was so drunk.

"You are in no shape for a fuck, Deon." Joaquin held him upright and walked into the lobby. "Where am I taking you?"

"Third floor." Deon removed his wallet and looked for the hotel key. He handed it to Joaquin and dropped his wallet trying to put it back. Joaquin picked it up and placed it into Deon's back pocket. "Good thing I am not the type to take advantage." Joaquin poked the elevator call button.

"I am lost, Joaquin. Lost." Deon became emotional.

"Okay. Quiet. Shh." He helped Deon onto the elevator and pushed the button for the third floor.

Deon leaned on Joaquin and began to feel weepy from his exhaustion and inebriation.

"Which room?" Joaquin asked when they arrived at the floor.

"This way." Deon stumbled and gripped tightly to Joaquin. He stopped and pointed.

Joaquin slid the card in and out of the metal box; a green light lit and Joaquin opened the door. Deon tried to walk in on his own and went down to his knees.

"Jesus Christ, Deon!" Joaquin hauled him up, allowing the door to shut behind them with a bang and Joaquin located the bedroom and carried Deon to it. "I have never seen you like this."

Deon was made to sit on the bed and Joaquin began taking off Deon's shoes, preparing him for sleep.

"I have lost him." Deon moaned and glanced up at the air duct which had been replaced after the camera was removed. "Lost him."

170

"You don't get your cock sucked by a senator's son and expect him not to leave you." Joaquin nudged Deon flat on the bed and undid his belt and trousers.

"How was I to know!" Deon covered his face and whined, "How was I to know..."

Joaquin tugged off Deon's slacks and then worked on his shirt. "If you need to throw up, warn me."

"I am not sick to my stomach. My heart is broken." Deon began to wail.

"You just met this man!" Joaquin took Deon's shirt off and tried to get him under the covers of the bed. "Why? Why is he so wonderful?"

Deon curled into a ball and felt hot tears run down his cheek to the pillow. "I wish I knew."

"It's the power. You are drunk on his power. Hmm? I man who could be the next president? Is that why?" Joaquin rubbed Deon's back.

"No. It's more than that. He doesn't flaunt the power. He's modest. You should see the certificates in his home office. He is a war hero, a scholar..."

"And in love with a crazy French model who was stupid enough to have sex with the son. How old was this young man? Legal?"

"Yes!" Deon thought about it. "Oh, no. I assume he was. He must have been."

"Deon."

"Yes. He looked like he was. I don't know." Deon rolled over to gaze at Joaquin. "Have I deflowered an underage youth?"

"You tell me."

Deon covered his face. "He will never forgive me. Never!"

"Quiet. I can't leave you like this. I can call Clair."

Deon stopped Joaquin from calling her. "It is two in the morning. Please. Leave Clair alone. She has enough work."

"Will you be okay?" Joaquin caressed Deon's cheek.

171

"Can you stay? Watch over me?"

Joaquin checked his phone for the time.

"It's Sunday tomorrow." Deon frowned, and reached for him.

"Yes. And I have to pack to leave for Paris."

"An hour? At least? Until I sleep?"

Joaquin took off his shoes and sat beside Deon on the bed, leaning on the headboard. He picked up the television remote and Deon rested his head on Joaquin's lap as Joaquin surfed channels.

"Thank you, dear friend."

"You rest. You will be sick if you don't lay still."

Deon closed his eyes and all he could think about was David. "*Mon dieu…*"

Deon heard his friend's exclamation and looked at the large TV. It was showing a twenty-four hour news channel and the coverage was of David's wife's home and speculation as to what was going on inside.

"No." Deon tried to sit up, inching his way so he was wedged against the pillows beside Joaquin.

"This is not good." Joaquin set the remote down as they both listened to the talking heads.

'*…rumor is they have arrested the senator's son, but the police are being very tight-lipped about why…*'

'*And as we speak an apartment where Jim Asher had been staying has been raided and as you can see computer equipment is being removed…*'

Deon moaned and held onto Joaquin as he witnessed a split screen, one with police taking items from an apartment house, and the other of police cars keeping back reporters at a private residence.

'*…it is obvious the senator has been the target of a vicious slander campaign after being seen with Deon Gael, a French fashion model…*"

Deon choked and Joaquin held onto him tighter.

172

'...*what we are trying to determine is if it was his son who was undermining his father's hopes of being selected as the next candidate for the White House...and if so, why?*'

"Why would a son do this to his father?" Joaquin asked.

"I am sick. I have been used. I feel as if I am in a nightmare."

Joaquin rubbed Deon to comfort him. "How could you know? Don't blame yourself."

"Don't blame myself?" Deon shouted. "I allowed a stranger in a bellhop uniform to suck my cock! Then did nothing but submit when he forced me into a sexual act. I am a fool."

"Stop...You were the victim." Joaquin kissed Deon's hair.

Deon stared at the broadcast which had a reader-board running under it of each tweet that had been sent to derail David's campaign hopes. It was like watching a train wreck. Deon simply could not look away.

Chapter 14

David held his son until he settled down and then shifted away from him so Jim had space and could gather his thoughts.

Jim blew his nose on a tissue and wiped his eyes. "I'm sorry, Dad."

David felt his stress flow out of him like a balloon poked with a pin. "I accept your apology."

His eyes red from his tears and the exhaustion, Jim turned on the sofa and looked at David. "It's hard growing up in your shadow."

David kept quiet, thinking about his own ambition to fill his father's shoes and constantly make the man proud. Which he had done with an enormous amount of work.

Jim wiped at his nose with the tissue. "I flunked out of school."

David winced and had no idea and wondered if Lydia knew. He kept quiet.

"I couldn't concentrate on anything. I kept seeing you on TV looking so big and powerful...as if like a superhero. And I was barely able to make a 'C' let alone get awards or do extra work."

Heartsick about his son's struggles, David had so many questions to ask Jim, but didn't.

"...so I dropped out. I didn't want Mom to know, so I stayed with my friend Greg most of the time. He has an apartment by your house." Jim inhaled and picked at a hangnail as if he couldn't find the courage to meet his father's gaze. "Then, I was at the fashion show when you met Deon, bored and spying on you. I saw the way you two looked at each other. And I thought, there he is, Mr Perfect, about to get a gorgeous model…"

David was sure now his son was gay or bi. He withheld comment, his fingers interlaced on his lap as murmurs continued to come from the kitchen.

"So…so I got jealous of that too." Jim rubbed at his nose. "You had, like, everything I always wanted. You know? You're smart, you're tall and handsome, you always seem to fight for what's right…spend all your time helping people…then you came out and I thought, oh, finally! You'll feel the bullshit I did. But…" Jim finally looked at David. "You didn't. You were applauded as brave and strong. And everyone rallied around you to see you become the first out gay president. How can I compete with that?"

"Why do you feel you have to? I have never belittled you. Never told you negative things. All through your youth I have been there for you. Praised everything you have done."

Jim didn't reply.

"And so has your mother. We don't have any unreal expectations for you or Veronica. You both will find your own way in your life, and both of us are here to help you or guide you."

"But it didn't work that way."

David waited for his explanation.

Jim looked at the floor and appeared frustrated. "You're busy. Always doing something. And Mom is too. She's constantly out leading some cause or heading a committee. And Veronica is of course a straight 'A' student. I'm the fuckup."

"You are not a fuckup. But you made terrible choices. And forcing a man to have sex is illegal, Jimmy. Of all the acts that you have done, that is the one I am most upset about. How could you do that to Deon?"

"I just thought you being with that cute guy…it wasn't fair. I could never get a man like that to fall for me."

175

"Jimmy, you're only nineteen. I'm forty-seven. It took me a very long time to meet a nice guy."

Jim met his father's eyes again.

"And you can be a decent man. A nice man, although...the shaved head and shirt make you look like a street punk." David tried not to get too angry. "You could join the Navy and fit right in with that head."

Jim chuckled.

David touched his hand. "I had no idea you were suffering. I mean that. And if you want me to drop out of the race I will, so we can have more time to do things."

Jim appeared shocked. "You'd do that for me?"

"Yes."

David could see the wheels turning in Jim's head. "All you have to do, Jimmy, is ask me. I can't read minds. And you have to go to counseling. And I want you to formally apologize to Deon and swear to me you will never make another person submit without consent." David was struggling on how to deal with that incident, since forgiveness was a hard pill for him to swallow. "So? Do you want me to give up on the run for president?"

"No."

"No." David tilted his head.

"I want you to run. I want you to be the first out gay president."

"I doubt I will be. But thanks for the endorsement."

"I'll take everything down from the 'net. Promise. I'll apologize in public and to Deon. If Eric wants, he can have a news conference and I'll be there."

"You'd do that for me?" David asked.

Jim shifted on the sofa. "Yeah. I will."

David opened his arms.

Jim fell against him and held him.

"I love you, Jimmy. You know I do. But you have to begin acting like a civilized man."

"I love you too, Dad. I'm so fucking sorry."

"Okay, it's done. Okay? We can do what we can to fix it, and get you back on track." David moved so he could see Jim's face. "If you don't like college, what do you want to do?"

"I wouldn't mind being in a band."

David laughed. "Do you play an instrument?"

"The drums. I'm getting better."

"Do you want to go to music school?"

"Yeah?" Jim's eyes lit up.

"Sure." David shrugged. "I don't see why you can't pursue what your dream job is."

"I thought you'd be so mad. So disappointed in me."

"Why? That's what I don't get. What have I ever done in the past to make you believe I would not support you?"

Jim took a moment to reflect. "Maybe it wasn't anything you did, but it was the life you've led. Those medals, the degrees...I thought the son of Senator David Asher would be scrutinized if he turned out to be a lowly drummer."

"Then that was in your head. Not from me."

"It was."

Eric peeked into the room. "It sounds as if things are going well in here."

David stood up. "They are. Jimmy wants to be a drummer in a band. I think we need to find him a music school, Eric." David made sure his expression was clear to Eric that he should not express negative thoughts.

"If that's what our Jimmy wants, it's what he'll get."

"Are you hungry?" David asked his son.

"Kinda. But it's, like, three in the morning."

"Go see what your mom has for you to snack on."

Jim stood, and with his head low, as if ashamed, he walked by Eric and David into the kitchen.

David brought Eric out of the hearing range of the three in the kitchen.

"We need to make a statement to the press," Eric said, "The whole family together. Do you think Jimmy would apologize in public?"

"He said he would." David thought about Deon and took his phone out of his pocket.

"Let me speak to Leona. She's been out there with those vultures." Eric walked to the front door.

David watched him go, and was about to dial Deon's number, when his whole family surrounded him.

Lydia was holding onto Jimmy and Veronica hugged David. "We're here for ya, Dad. What do you want us to do?"

"Eric is checking with Leona to see what's going on with the media. I'm afraid to turn on a TV."

"Dad?" Jim asked.

"Yes?"

"Let me say something to them. Let me tell them it was me."

"You would do that for me?" David asked.

"Yeah. I would."

Veronica teased her little brother, "See? He's not too much of a fuckup!"

Lydia shook her head. "Language? This is supposed to be a family of class."

They all looked at each other and cracked up with laughter at the irony. David dabbed at his eyes at the comment. "Oh, Christ. I'm sorry, Lydia, but that is too funny considering the last three days."

She wiped at her eyes as she was caught in a laughing fit of her own making. "I know. I swear, we must be one of the most dysfunctional families in the country."

"I wouldn't go quite that far." David contained his laughter and went for a group hug. He held onto his family and closed his eyes. "I love all of you. You have no idea."

Lydia and Veronica kissed his cheek and Jim gave him a shy smile.

"Now," Veronica said, "Go out and get your man!"

"Not yet. We still have some unfinished business. We're going to make a statement to the press."

Lydia said, "Oh! Let me change." She rushed off.

Veronica looked down at her shorts and top. "Am I okay?"

"You're fine." David kissed her forehead.

Jim gave his father a sheepish glance.

"Yeah, kid, the Anarchist Tee has to go." He winked.

"I can turn it inside out."

"And the piercings!" Veronica said, "Yeck."

"Leave him alone." David gave his daughter a warning look as Jim turns his shirt inside out and put it on. He actually took both piercings out and said. "Got a wig?"

Veronica held her stomach and roared with laughter as David shook his head. "You're a chip off the old block, kiddo." He held Jim and shook him.

"Oh, God, I'm dying." Veronica dabbed her eyes. "Let me see if my mascara is running." She walked away.

David cupped his son's jaw. "For you, my door is always open. You know that, right?"

"Thanks, Dad." Jim took a minute and said, "And...I think I may be gay."

"That's my man." David hugged him. "Be brave. Be who you are."

"You think Deon has a friend to set me up with?"

David choked on a laugh and said, "Probably not." *I think Deon wants to kill you.* "You do realize how you treated him, right? I mean, I don't know if Deon will ever forgive you, and I'm struggling with that issue myself."

Jim nodded. "It was fucked up. I should be punished."

"Well, Deon may want to kick your ass, but I have no idea what to do with you. Maybe you need to volunteer in a soup kitchen, do some community service or get sex offender therapy."

"Yikes."

"Yeah, that's how serious I am taking that event, Jimmy. I'm struggling to believe my son would ever force a man to do anything against his will."

Jimmy covered his face.

"If you ever do something like that again, I will make sure you spend time in jail."

Under his breath Jim said, "To get gang-raped and beat up."

"No. To understand the magnitude of what you did to a very kind intelligent man."

Tears ran from Jim's eyes. "He'll never forgive me. You won't either."

"I won't say never, but I will say how tough it will be for both of us to forget what you did."

"I'm sorry. I don't know what else I can do."

David nodded and waited for his family to get ready for the press.

~

Nodding off on Joaquin's shoulder, Deon was startled when Joaquin pointed to the television, making the volume louder. "Look! It is the senator!"

Deon sat up and tried to focus through his foggy stupor. David, a pretty woman in a pink pants suit, a younger woman in a top and shorts, and...the freak who had trapped Deon in the men's room at the restaurant and sucked his dick in the last hotel, were standing together in front of the press that had been gathered outside the residence.

"That is the young man?" Joaquin asked.

"With his head shaven. Disgraceful." Deon sneered and held Joaquin's hand as it looked as if David was going to address the press.

180

POWER PLAY

Lights from cameras flashed and David appeared to withstand the pressure and comments and questions thrown at him. An older man, who the media called David's chief of staff, stood in front of the family and held up his hand for quiet. "The senator and his family have a quick statement which hopefully will put all this to rest. Then, it is my hope you will leave him and his family in peace." The older man gestured to David.

David stepped closer to the press, surrounded by his wife and children and held onto them. "I want to apologize to the American public for the last few days. Terrible slander has hit an innocent man, Deon Gael, a kind and giving French model that is in Washington for a fundraising event."

Deon gasped and covered his mouth, having no idea he would be mentioned.

"Mr Gael's perfect reputation was tarnished because of his association with me. And to set the record straight between Mr Gael and myself, yes, I have dated him and will continue to, if that is what Mr Gael wishes."

"I wish! I wish!" Deon got to his knees and moved closer to the television.

"This unfortunate event all could have been prevented if I had been a better father to my son, Jim." David held onto the young man. "Unknown to me, Jim has been the victim of bullying because I came out."

Deon growled, "Victim? He is perpetrator!" He spat in disgust. "Pig!"

"Shh." Joaquin made the volume louder.

"...and sadly, he lashed out. Jim is very sorry for any of the harm he may have caused to me or to Mr Gael."

Deon ground his jaw as he watched David gesture to the young man to speak.

The young man looked as if he had been crying, his eyes were puffy and his face flushed. "I...I want to apologize to my Dad and to Mr Gael. I...I acted worse than the bullies that

181

tormented me. And I am very sorry. Please nominate my dad for the presidency. He is a great guy with a lot of love and forgiveness in his heart." The young man lowered his head and backed up.

The chief of staff stopped any question as the press began to hammer them, and said, "It's late, ladies and gentlemen, and I thank you for allowing the Asher family to speak. They have no more comments, and it would be appreciated if this ordeal could be placed behind all of us as a terrible misunderstanding. Goodnight."

Deon watched as the cameras panned to the family returning to the residence.

"So?" Joaquin asked. "That is that."

Deon sank back on the bed and tried to think.

Joaquin looked at him. "He said he is sorry. If you expect roses from a young screwed up man, you are going to be let down."

"No." Deon curled into the pillow. "I don't expect that. I expect David to never contact me again."

"His words say he will." Joaquin leaned down to kiss Deon's cheek. "Let me go now. I will fall asleep in your bed if I don't get to my hotel."

Deon laid his head on Joaquin's lap and held him. "Five more minutes. Until I can rest."

Joaquin petted him gently. "Deon, there is no sense in getting into a state. You don't want this man. He is so complex. Look," Joaquin gestured to the aftermath of the television pundits starting the debate about what was said with rebuttals from both sides of the political spectrum. "You want to be far away from this. He has child who is a rapist, screwed up in the head, an ex-wife, scandal...why do you need that?"

Deon closed his eyes and tried to agree with Joaquin. Why would he need that? And David and he will have a long distance relationship.

What is the point? Not only that. Although the creep had apologized, Deon wanted to kick his ass.

~

"Goodnight, David." Lydia kissed his cheek.

"Goodnight, Veronica."

"'Night, Dad."

David looked at his son as they all stood in the living room.

"I'm really sorry, Dad."

"Come here." David opened his arms.

Jim hugged him and closed his eyes.

David kissed the top of his shaven head. "I'm here. Okay?"

He felt Jim nod and released him.

"Are you going to be okay?" Lydia asked David.

"I won't know until later in the week. I expect some fallout, and if they want me to drop out of the race, I will."

David walked with Eric to the door and were guarded by security to their cars as the press either continued to linger, and even more amazing, some actually left.

Eric stopped David before David entered his car. "I'll keep an eye on the polls."

"Don't worry, Eric. It was a long shot. And I'm happy to be a senator."

Eric patted David's arm and headed to his car with his driver.

David sat in the back seat of the sedan and his driver asked, "Home, sir?"

"No. The hotel Deon is staying at."

"Yes, sir."

"And you don't have to hang around. I think we figured out the threat."

"Up to you, sir." The driver left the media vans behind as he drove off.

"I'll take a private limo back to my house. Thanks, though."

The man nodded and drove David to the hotel.

David looked at his phone. All the tweets had vanished, the site had been taken down, and nothing appeared on the social media any longer that exploited the nightmare he and Deon had just endured, and that included, them being aware that Deon had sexual acts with both his son and him. At least that horror had not been leaked.

As he scanned the text messages he missed, his press secretary stated all the electronics from the young man's apartment had been confiscated and the offending videos and files, deleted.

David texted her '*thank you*'.

The driver pulled up to the front lobby entrance and David handed him cash.

"No, but thank you, sir. We aren't allowed to accept tips."

"Okay. Well, your work was appreciated, not to mention the discretion of the whole team."

"Our pleasure, sir. Good luck with the election."

"Thanks." David got out of the back of the sedan and entered the lobby as it drove off. He rode the elevator to the third floor and tapped lightly on Deon's hotel door, not knowing if he was asleep or not. It was nearing three a.m.

The door opened and when David saw it was Joaquin his fury hit immediately.

And as if Joaquin could read it on David's face, Joaquin held up his hand and said, "He got drunk. No sex. Just brought him here."

"David?" Deon called from the other room.

David waited, suspicious as hell.

Deon rushed to him, wearing just briefs while Joaquin was fully dressed.

"Now you are together, I may take my leave." Joaquin said something to Deon in French and opened the hotel door.

Deon replied to Joaquin and then as Joaquin left, he looked at David until the hotel door closed behind Joaquin.

"We watched media frenzy. David. Do you forgive me? I am so overwhelm with pain." Deon touched him.

"Joaquin?" David pointed to the door. "You invited him to your hotel room?"

"No." Deon tried to hold David's hand but he resisted. "I was in bar, near…" Deon pointed in the direction. "I no have no one to cry on. I call him. He come and have to make sure I can get here, since I had too many." Deon could see the fire in David's eyes. "David. I no cheat. No." Deon crossed his finger over his heart. "I do nothing but cry for you. You believe?"

David was dead on his feet. If he was honest with himself, he no longer had any fight left in him. He began to walk to the bedroom where he could hear the television spouting the latest update on his story. He looked at the bed, then the nightstand. There was no evidence a sexual act took place and if Joaquin had been naked, he was quite the quick change artist.

"You come to say goodbye, yes?" Deon sat on the bed, one leg under him, and reached for David.

David loosened his tie and toed off his shoes. "I came to stay with you, but only if it's okay."

"Yes!" Deon hugged him. "I am misery watching unfold. How can son do this to you? To me?"

David continued to undress as Deon touched him, caressed him. "Because he's confused. He feels as if he has to somehow compete with me." David stood and took off his dress slacks and then draped his clothing over a chair. Once he was in briefs, he entered the bathroom to splash his face.

Deon appeared in the mirror's reflection. "Is hard. How can son ever step into your footsteps? You are amazing man."

"And a crappy dad."

"No!" Deon held a towel for David and he dried his face with it. David returned to the bed, picked up the remote and shut off the television. He crawled into the bed, and Deon was right

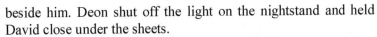

beside him. Deon shut off the light on the nightstand and held David close under the sheets.

"You can sleep. In my arms." Deon drew closer.

"I can. I'm completely drained." David held onto him, closing his eyes.

"Yes. Drained. But we see what tomorrow brings, you and I."

"Yeah. But if I think about it, I won't sleep."

"Then think about this, David." Deon pressed his lips against David's. "My love for you."

David scooped Deon into his arms and held onto him, finally closing his eyes and falling asleep.

POWER PLAY

Chapter 15

David opened his eyes.

Sunday morning light was filtering into the window which was covered by a very heavy curtain to block it out.

Beside him was a French fashion model, asleep, facing him, his beard growth dark on his jaw.

David crushed the pillow under his head and stared at Deon while he slept. The night had been draining and he didn't want to think about Jim having forced 'his' man to have sex. David tried to be the type of individual to turn the page. Move on. Dwelling on this type of shit could eat him up alive.

He had failed somewhere in his son's life, but had hopes that from today on, he could be there for Jimmy, let him follow his dreams of music and drumming, and support him in whatever his decisions to come may be. And, get the kid much needed help. Jim was sick to have done what he did to Deon.

What more could a parent do? Just be there when they fall, wipe their tears, and tell them, 'things will get better if you try'.

In reality, what Jim had done to him and Deon, was not 'okay'. But what was David supposed to do? Anything other than love and forgiveness would be seen as a blight on his record, and as his father had always taught him, 'Just come clean'. And being honest? Telling the public Jim was a vile pig who has forced Deon into a sexual act? Was he supposed to slap Jim, kick the crap out of him and still be seen as 'presidential' material? Yes, he did want to punish Jim, make him see what he had done was not some minor act. But it all came back to him. If

187

he hit Jim, sent him to jail or to a camp for troubled kids, how would that reflect on him? He had no choice. It was selfish to not punish Jim for his disgusting acts but…in reality, somehow David had failed as a parent.

And as long as the video and information that both father and son had screwed the same man did not surface, David tried not to feel that crappy pit in his stomach that perhaps, this was not his year to see the inside of the White House. He was young. There was always the next four years.

David looked at the long dark eyelashes that surrounded Deon's eyes, admiring his beauty. Yeah, maybe he was smitten with Deon's great looks, but if the man was an ass, those looks would soon lose their appeal. Truth was, Deon was fabulous inside as well. And as a lover? David could not wish for a better fuck.

As his thoughts turned carnal in nature, David's cock grew hard. He picked up the sheet and slowly lowered it down Deon's body, so he could see his man nude.

He then held himself, and gently played as he stared at a man he was dying to screw.

Then as if Deon sensed something through his slumber, his eyes opened and David was treated to those lovely sky blue irises.

Deon came around from the deep sleep and rubbed his eyes and face, then realized his entire body was exposed and David was holding his stiff cock.

Deon laughed softly and gave David a sexy smile. "The lion is awaken."

"Just looking at you gets me hot." David pulled on his cock, which was stiff and a drop of pre-cum appeared at the slit.

Deon scooted closer, pecked David's lips and then lowered down on the bed.

As he did, David flopped to his back and felt the tickling kisses trace down his torso to his cock.

Deon enveloped David's dick and held it in his hot wet mouth.

David moaned and spread his legs, and bent his knees.

After giving David a good sucking, Deon leaned up and asked, "What do you want? Hmm? Continue here, or make love to your lamb?"

"Make love."

Dion licked the head of David's dick and threw him a kiss as he closed himself into the bathroom. David held his cock, feeling it was still wet from Deon's mouth. He jerked it to keep it hard as he thought about screwing Deon. Intruding thoughts tried to destroy the mood, but David made sure they did not interfere. He was going to fuck 'his' man.

He glanced around the room and spotted his clothing on a chair. David peeked at the closed bathroom door, then stood and slipped his belt out of the slacks he wore, and brought it with him to the bed. He sat up against the headboard and looped the belt, imagining taking Deon while he was tied up.

A rush of pure sexual pleasure washed over David at the thought. Power. It was intoxicating, even in bed.

After Deon prepared himself he exited the bathroom with the condoms and lubrication in his hand and stopped short when he spotted the belt.

"My lover have something kink in mind?" He placed the items he carried onto the nightstand and then held his wrists together.

David looped the belt around them and tightened it up. Deon's cock swelled and David forced Deon to kneel on the bed, tying the belt tightly around his wrists.

"Your turn to not speak nor move." David knelt behind him.

Deon moaned and rested his head on his hands, his ass high in the air.

David caressed his hips and thighs gently, admiring Deon's perfect build. David climbed off the bed and stepped into the bathroom, he quickly rinsed his mouth with mouthwash to freshen it up, then noticed a brush. David gave his reflection a wicked grin.

~

Deon knew now, there was nothing stopping them. Whatever had happened was no longer today. It was yesterday, and today was indeed, a new day.

Deon spotted David coming from the bathroom, not hiding what he was holding. Deon stifled a laugh and said, "We need buy dildo, yes?"

A slap hit Deon's bottom and David said, "Did I say you can speak?"

Deon began chewing on the leather belt in anticipation of being fucked by an object. *I give, now I receive. Yes, I am teaching him well.*

Slick gel, cool to the touch, made Deon shiver. David gently circled his ass and then pushed the tip of his finger inside him.

Deon shivered and closed his eyes, resting his forehead into the pillow and his teeth clamped on the leather.

As David explored Deon, first with his fingers, then with the brush handle against Deon's rim, Deon held back a groan and clenched his fists.

The brush handle was used to penetrate Deon's ass and Deon wanted to beg for David's cock to replace it. He crushed the pillows against the headboard and felt like shredding them from the mixture of pain and pleasure.

David removed the brush and a warm soft cock replaced it. Immediately Deon relaxed and David's cock slipped in easily. Deon allowed the belt to drop from his teeth and began moving with David's rhythm, now, finally feeling the friction internally that the brush did not provide. His cock responded and Deon bit back a whimper of pleasure.

David held Deon's hips and made his way deeper until Deon could feel David's body against his own. David reached between them and held their balls together, pressing them so they touched.

Deon writhed on the bed, looking between his legs at David's powerful straddle and seeing David playing with Deon's cock and balls as he fucked him.

Deon's breathing began to heighten as his passion grew, and the spark of a climax kept striking.

Balling his fists in the confines of the belt, Deon pushed back, meeting David's thrusts.

"Oh, fuck…"

Deon heard what usually preceded David coming and chills washed up his spine. He began moving more quickly on David's cock, wanting to come.

David suddenly was not in control and held onto Deon as Deon began to take over. He thrust back deep and hard, then let David's cock draw to the tip, before pushing backwards and going deep once more.

"Deon…fucking hell!"

Deon knelt up, his hands still bound, and sat on David's lap, hopping up and down on David's cock.

David grunted and Deon felt him come and heard David's moans get caught in his throat. Deon grabbed his own cock and jerked it, still riding David for the internal friction and when he came he prevented throwing back his head and not hitting David in the face, but leaned back on his shoulder and shot his cum all over the sheets.

David wrapped his arms around Deon and held him, catching his breath.

Deon sank on David's cock and felt it throb deeply inside him. "So in love…" Deon moaned.

After the orgasmic swoon, David untied the belt, freeing Deon's hands. Deon, reached for David, and while their bodies were still united, he kissed him.

David moaned as if delirious and as the kisses became mad and passionate, Deon moved and David's cock slipped out. Deon faced his man and cupped his jaw, straddling David's knees, their sweat making their contact slick and David's pubic hair was sticky with gel against Deon's, which was slick with cum.

They stayed that way, kissing, caressing and recovering from the climax high, and Deon didn't want to stop or for their passion to end.

But what was going to happen when he went back to Paris and David began his campaign and debates?

Deon did not know. But he knew one thing. He was now here. In Washington DC, making love to one of the most amazing, powerful men in the world.

And he wouldn't have traded that precious time with David for anything he owned.

~

As the climax high subsided and their kissed became puffs of air from their heavy breathing, David caressed Deon's jaw and asked, "When do you leave?"

"Tomorrow."

David nodded.

"When do you come to Paris?"

David smiled and kissed Deon. "I don't know."

"Then?"

David searched Deon's gaze. "You keep saying you love me."

"I do. So much." Deon interlaced his fingers and held them near his own heart.

"How much are you willing to sacrifice to be here? In DC?"

"All, David. All."

David was stunned. "All? Your career?"

"I speak to Joaquin about this just subject. Mark Antonious...he has model contract with U.S. products. If I can find agent, I too, can model here."

"Is there such an agency? Here? In DC? I would think New York or LA."

"Yes, Joaquin say same, but I must find."

"You would be willing to do that for me? To stay here?"

"Of course! Why you not see in me truth?"

David wondered, if Deon stayed, would his son react badly? And was David going to avoid a male lover for his son? For politics? Forever?

"You want me stay?" Deon asked, appearing afraid.

"Yes. Hell yes." David cupped Deon's jaw. "But I have no idea if you can get that kind of work, or if living with my beautiful French model will be acceptable."

"So much to think of. So much." Deon ran his finger down David's chest to the spent condom. "And all we have is two men in love. So? I always have conflict in mind why so many care badly."

"You're not the only one." David glanced at his cock going soft in the rubber. "Let me get this off." David climbed out of the bed and headed to the bathroom.

He tossed out the condom and Deon started the shower.

David looked at them both in the mirror. Two men in love. To some; a thing of beauty, to others; a sin and a travesty.

To his son?

David had no idea how Jim would react if this relationship with Deon took a step closer and became a live-in lover...

Deon stepped into the shower and reached for him. David joined him and under the spray they held each other, kissing and knowing life simply was not easy, never showed a clear path, and sometimes didn't always go as one wished.

But they were not ordinary men.

No.

They were powerful men. And those who did nothing but let others decide their future, played a very sad game.

It was about love. Not war. Not sex.

Love.

And David believed, love conquered hate. He had seen it in fifty states, one by one they fell, and hate was defeated, defeated to the point where the American public was actually considering voting for an out gay man to be their next leader.

If they couldn't accept David as the man he was, then maybe he couldn't accept them either.

Deon leaned back and they met gazes.

David never thought he'd say it to a man, but he did. "I love you too."

Deon closed his eyes and embraced David, squeezing him and rocking him in his arms.

"You make me happiest man in the world, David. Happy. So happy."

David kissed Deon's wet neck and held onto him. The pursuit of happiness…it was everyone's right.

POWER PLAY

One week later....

"The next question for our potential candidate is for Senator Asher…"

David stood at a podium with the other men and women trying to gain the vote to represent their party in the upcoming election.

The commentator asked, "Senator, do you truly believe the country is ready to elect an out gay man with a French lover, to be the next president of the United States?"

David had been hit with this question continuously. "I hope the American people can see me as just a man. A man with the same goals as the other members of my party. I knew in my lifetime we would see a minority as president, and I am hoping a woman as well. We evolve as humans. We learn to see beyond labels to the person underneath. I am hoping my record in the military and in my political career is their guide, and not who I decide to date."

One of his opposing candidates said, "Sadly, who you date is a major part of who you are. And a fashion model?" the man said, as sarcastically as he could. After all, they were all vying for the same position.

Slander and mudslinging had become the way of life for politics.

David checked on their moderator who nodded, allowing David to respond to the comment. "Senator," David addressed his opponent, "Judging Deon Gael as simply a 'fashion model' is naïve. Mr Gael is a brilliant man of the world. One smart enough to use his beauty to earn a living. And you are telling me I should be ashamed of that? Shall we compare partners and see which has the better resume?"

A rumble of laughter was heard in the audience.

The woman candidate put in her two cents, against David. "It's obvious, Senator, what you are doing is influencing your children. That alone should tell you a man like you has no place in the oval office."

The moderator didn't hesitate to give David the nod to reply.

David looked at the woman candidate. "Out of all the individuals running, Ms Governor, I expected better from you. My son was bullied because I am gay. What better way to prevent this type of anonymous abuse than to prove to the world there is no difference between a man, straight or gay, or bi, or…a woman."

A little argument broke out between candidates about the topic, but David remained quiet. He wasn't about to get into a pissing match.

The moderator stopped it and said, "Shall we move on? I think Senator Asher has answered your questions…"

David stood tall as the next person who wanted the coveted job was asked about what he would do about unemployment.

As David listened he looked out into the crowd, trying to judge whether he'd earned their respect, or simply put, the world was not ready for a gay man to be elected.

The longer the debate wore on, the less David cared. Ambition had been strong in David. All his life he strived for goals that most people didn't think were attainable.

David had tried to change the world, right the wrongs and fight for the weak. He had a little impact. But it was never enough.

As his lover was struggling to gain employment permanently in Washington DC, David began to lose interest in the arguing going on between members of his own party. This was only the beginning. Once the party had selected a representative, then the battle would intensify against the opposing party. That war would be so ugly, it would be the fodder for twenty-four hour news channels and comedy networks to mock and battle over.

And after a week without Deon, trying to get Jim into a place in his life where he could feel happy and whole, into counseling and sex offender treatment, David wondered if his power play, this jump to try and get the top job in politics, was simply no longer his dream.

"Senator?" the commentator tried to get David's attention.

He snapped back into focus and said, "I believe in the voters. I believe in their strength, their values. Debating over my personal life, trying to justify why I am who I am…is not my way. To close this topic, hopefully once and for all, I am here to serve. If I am selected to be your candidate, I assure you you will get the best of me. And if not, I will support whomever the citizens of this country decide will be their next leader."

Silence fell on the candidates and the audience at the unexpected announcement.

David said quietly, "I have fought enough battles; in war, and trying to convert ignorance into open-mindedness. But that is no longer my battle. My record stands for itself. If you want me, I am here. If not…I am very content to keep serving as a senator." David scanned the quiet crowd. "Thank you."

Applause broke out and David noticed his competition appeared slightly stunned. After all, this was supposed to be war, not a waving of the white flag. But David was war weary.

As a matter of fact…

I'm done.

~

Deon exited the private car in front of the hotel, the one near David's home residence. He hadn't told David he was returning to Washington for an interview and wanted to surprise him. No there were not a lot of agencies in DC, but there were a few. And Deon, with his international attention, some created by the 'scandal' began to get invitations to come in for interviews.

Deon did not say goodbye to Clair and his fashion agency yet. No. Not until he had a signed contract.

He was helped with his luggage to the lobby and met the man behind the desk to confirm his reservation and get his key.

The clerk took Deon's credit cards, read his passport and handed him a card key. "Would you like help with your luggage?"

"*Oui.* That would be appreciated."

The clerk nodded to a bellboy and Deon tipped his driver and followed the young man to the elevator, trying not to think of the bad times behind him, and hoping the best was yet to come.

He was shown to a room on the same floor he had stayed at previously but not the same room. The bellboy opened the door for Deon and gestured for him to enter.

The television was on, lights were lit and the young man set Deon's luggage on a stand in the bedroom.

"Anything else I can get you, sir?"

"No. Will be fine." Deon handed him cash and the young man left. As Deon took off his shoes he looked at the television. It was David, in a debate, standing on a stage with other people; the room decorated in red, white and blue.

Stunned, Deon was drawn to it, standing in front of the enormous HD flat screen and heard David say, "I have fought enough battles; in war, and trying to convert ignorance into open-mindedness. But that is no longer my battle. My record stands for itself. If you want me, I am here. If not...I am very content to keep serving as a senator...Thank you."

Deon was struck silent at what sounded like a speech of defeat. He had not heard the entire debate, so he had no idea what David had been through.

He also didn't know if this was live or taped. He checked the time on his watch. It was five p.m. Washington time. Deon sent David a text. *'I am here.'*

Immediately one came back. *'You are where?'*

'Hotel where you last place me. I just arrive.'

Deon's phone rang.

"You're here?" David asked excitedly.

198

"Yes! You cannot be on TV and speaking at same time." Deon watched the screen.

"Are you watching the debate? That was earlier today. I'm home."

"Me come to you? Or you come to me?"

"Come here! Why are you in a hotel? Why didn't you tell me you were coming?"

Deon was overwhelmed at his enthusiasm. "I did not know for sure how to proceed. I have several interviews. And yes, there are model agents here, not only New York."

"I'll send someone to pick you up. Deon! You're here!"

"Yes! One week. You believe I return? I hope immigrations man will not think badly." Deon laughed.

"Don't unpack. On my way."

"Yes. Good. I just arrive." Deon looked at his luggage. "Meet in lobby? Or too public?"

"In the lobby. There's no more hiding, Deon. I'm through with this charade."

Deon didn't quite understand but said, "Okay. Lobby."

"Bye."

He hung up, looked at the television, saw David's expression, which was not happy, and to Deon appeared as if he was withdrawing, not fighting any longer. He slipped his shoes back on, and carried his shoulder bag on his arm, and wheeled his larger bag behind him, returning to the lobby.

~

David hustled out of his home and to a sedan with his driver there waiting. He had his cell phone to his ear as he sat in the backseat. He cupped the phone to tell the driver Deon's hotel name. Then he went back to his call. "Eric, I know I sounded defeated, but maybe I am."

"David! After all this?"

199

"Yes. Exactly. All this. This has been an awakening for me as well as my son, the public, and whoever else has been following this story."

"No, David, you can't back out of the race. The polls—"

"The polls! The polls!" David threw up his hand as they drove through Friday evening traffic. "They can shove the poll up their ass."

"You have no idea what a disappointment this is going to be to so many people, David."

"Look, next time. Four years from now. Okay? This scandal will be history, and the chances anyone knows about Deon getting attacked by Jimmy will have vanished..."

"David..."

"Eric," David said, rubbing his eyes. "I have already given my whole life to the public. I am almost fifty. Please."

A sigh preceded, "Well, I can't stop you."

"No. You can't. And I want to be off of the radar until I know if this thing with Deon is real or just a passing fancy."

"How will you figure that out? Didn't he fly back to Paris?"

As the car pulled up to the lobby of the hotel, David could see Deon waiting inside. He covered the phone and told his driver, "Help that man with his luggage and into the car."

"Yes, sir."

David got back on the phone. "No, Eric, he's here. Back in DC trying to find a modeling agency that's local."

"Here?"

"Here. Now. I am looking straight at him." David watched Deon's smile at the driver as he carried his shoulder bag and the man put his luggage into the trunk.

"Eric, let me find a little happiness...just for me."

"We'll talk more, David. I know many people will be upset."

"Yes. And I know one who will be upset if I don't try to make this work. Me. Goodbye, Eric." David hung up the phone, opened the back door, got out, and opened his arms to his lover.

Deon handed off his shoulder bag and embraced David, kissing him, rocking him in his arms.

David gestured for Deon to get into the car and then tackled him, lying on the back seat on top of him. David heard his driver chuckle and the door of the sedan shut.

Deon laughed as David ran kisses all over his face. "I have no idea you missed me so much. Is one week, yes?"

"Home, sir?" the driver asked.

"Yes. Please." David ground his cock against Deon's. He whispered, "And you came back. One week, and here you are."

"I must." Deon shrugged. "What is life without my lion?"

David cupped the back of Deon's head and met his lips, swirling tongues and going crazy.

They kissed until the car stopped and the driver asked, "Sir?"

David parted from Deon's mouth and stared at him. "Get into my bed, you sexy lamb."

"*Ohh,* my…" Deon narrowed his eyes at David.

David climbed out of the backseat and reached his hand to Deon. He hauled his man out, grabbed Deon's ass hard, as he walked to his front door and the driver retrieved the bags from the trunk.

Once inside, the driver left the bags and shut the door, leaving the men alone.

David chased Deon to his bedroom, and Deon, laughing like a young man, playfully avoided David's groping until he was standing at the bed.

Both men, panting for breath, grinned wickedly at each other. David began to get undressed, as he watched Deon do the same.

This is where I need to be. Here. With my match, my mate.

Deon took off the last article of his clothing, and then opened his arms. "I await."

David hopped to take off his sock, and then dove on Deon, pinning him to the bed and rubbing his body all over his lover.

Deon sniffed David's neck and hummed. "*Dangereux?*"

"Yes, is it getting you excited?" David felt both their cocks throbbing and reached to set them upright, side by side.

"Of course! That's it its purpose." Deon cupped David's jaw and they stared into each other's eyes. "Is right…us…together. Yes?"

"Yes." David knew it had to be. Deon was struggling to be with him, and he was battling with himself to do the same.

"Is sure? We meant to be?" Deon pointed to himself.

"I'm sure. Are you sure?"

"Oh yes, David. No can be more sure."

David scooped Deon into his arms and rolled over so Deon was on top. Deon leaned on his elbows and caressed the hair on David's chest. "What will public say? Hmm? If I live here?"

"I don't care." David spread his legs and Deon fell between them.

"You care. You always man of power."

"No. I am not playing that power game now. I think I'm ready to be me. David Asher, the lover of Deon Gael, if he is ready for me."

"Lover? Or?" Deon smiled wickedly and walked his fingers up David's arm. "Possibly husband?"

A rush of excitement washed over David. He closed his eyes to savor that comment. Then opened his eyes. "Did you just propose to me?"

"Is crazy. No? So soon. And you with chance at president…silly of me to even mention. Forgive."

"Yes."

"Yes. Is silly."

David held Deon's arms. "No. Yes, I would love to marry you."

Deon blinked and appeared stunned. "But…"

David touched Deon's lips. "It can be a long engagement."

"Serious?"

"I am if you are." David caressed Deon's handsome face.

202

"I am more than serious. I get on one knee and beg."

David laughed. "There's no need. Besides, which one of us will be the one to get on one knee and ask? To hold out a ring?"

Deon got the joke and grinned. "Such power play, yes? Between two lions."

David kissed him and then stared at him again. "And then you won't have to worry about staying here. You will be my husband, so..."

"I am so disbelief of this!" Deon laughed. "So soon. And you have battle to win to be president."

"Maybe. Maybe not."

No?" Deon tilted his head and his smile vanished. "They say something? On the channel I watch? Something to insult you?"

"No. But I think I have done enough. I mean, I have been something to everyone, and nothing to myself. Do you know what I mean?"

"Yes. Sadly, I do. I feel very much as well. Give all outside. Nothing left inside."

David embraced Deon and rolled over again so he was on top. "I want to make love to you."

"Mm. You are my lion. Yes."

"Without condoms?" David asked, nibbling Deon's jaw.

"I have been true. I do not touch another. You?"

"Cross my heart." David drew his fingers over his chest.

"Will be first time for me, no protection."

"Really?" David leaned up to look down at Deon.

"You no believe?"

"No. I do believe. I'm just surprised."

"No. No take chance. Never trusted. You, I trust. You are such high integrity, even with so much power."

"Well." David nudged Deon, "Go get ready to play, gorgeous."

"You have what I need?" Deon stood off the bed and pointed to the bathroom.

"Yes. Under the sink vanity."

Deon smiled and said, "You go nowhere."

"Not a chance."

Deon closed himself into the bathroom.

David looked up at the ceiling and smiled.

~

Deon prepared himself for his lover, glad he slept on the plane and the reception from David was so enthusiastic. It reaffirmed his belief that they could make it as a couple, two men. Simple. Not allowing who they were or what they did to push them apart. Right?

Time would tell. Deon may be many things, but a seer of the future he was not. He could only gauge his own feelings for David, and see the same love reflected in David's eyes. Eyes of a man he knew was honest and had strong beliefs.

After cleansing, he showered and made sure he was perfect for David, then opened the bathroom door to see him relaxing, waiting, and then his beautiful smile.

David reached out for Deon. Deon clasped his hand and stretched out beside him on the bed. "I am ready for my lion."

As if he were touching an angel, David caressed Deon's cheek, and ran his fingertips down Deon's neck to his chest.

Deon melted at the touch and closed his eyes for a moment to savor the senses of everything he was experiencing.

David kissed his way down Deon's body to his cock and nuzzled in, inhaling Deon and crushing his lips against Deon's balls.

Deon moaned and bent his knees, straddling for his lover, and opening himself up.

David reached for the lubrication he has set out while Deon was in the bathroom and used it on himself this time. He jerked his cock while he stared at Deon, making Deon feel loved and attractive.

David picked up each of Deon's legs and placed them on his shoulders, then scooted closer, pointing his cock at Deon's ass.

Deon inched downward to meet him and when they connected, for the first time without a barrier between them, both men groaned in harmony and David kept still, holding Deon's legs.

Deon had so much love in his heart for this man, he never thought one lover could be enough. But a man like David? He was more than enough.

David gently pushed deeper, making them one, and Deon held onto David, encouraging him to not be shy and enjoy it.

David began panting from the excitement and once he was deep inside Deon he used his slick hands to excite Deon, running palm over fist over Deon's cock and bringing chills to Deon's skin.

"David...I love so much." Deon felt David's cock pulsate.

"I can't believe how good this feels." David held Deon's thighs and thrust inside him.

"You no hold back. You have pleasure." Deon touched himself, and when David took notice and his cock throbbed inside Deon, Deon continued to self-stimulate to excite his man.

"I can't hold back. Oh my God, without a condom it feels unbelievable." David's hip movement grew faster and deeper with his thrusts.

Deon stared at David's muscular chest, the hair on it, and the beauty of his powerful senator. He began to feel the climax rise in himself. He jerked on his cock and reached for David.

"Oh fuck..." David obviously could sense Deon was getting closer and pushed in deeply, threw back his head and gasped as he came.

Watching David's pure pleasure, Deon shivered and came as well, spattering his chest, milking his cock and awash with chills.

David pulled out, and leaned down, lapping the spent cum off Deon's skin. Deon moaned and went limp on the bed as David licked his skin and then collapsed on top of Deon, breathless and bathed in perspiration.

"We make love, pure love." Deon hugged David, kissing his cheek and neck.

"And...can I make an announcement?"

"Announce?" Deon asked, panting.

"To the press?"

"Of?"

"Our engagement?"

Deon brightened and smiled. "Yes! Of course! Will be fine for me, but for you?"

"I'll let my family know first. And..." David leaned all his weight on Deon, brushing over his lips with his own. "...let the rest be damned."

"You feel so strong?" Deon was both terrified David was ruining his career, and thrilled to be loved as much as he loved David.

"Yes. I do." David touched Deon's hair affectionately, brushing it off his sweaty brow.

Deon hugged him, wrapping his arms and legs around David, tears filling his eyes. "Never would I dream of this happiness. Is possible?"

"With two powerful guys like us?" David teased, "Let them try to stop us!"

Deon held David close, closing his eyes and whispering, "I love you so much. You simply do not know."

"I think I do. Deon, lover, I think I do."

POWER PLAY

Epilogue

David sipped champagne as he stared at a garden gone to hibernation near the chapel. The ring shouldn't feel odd on his finger since he had worn one for years, but this one felt different. As if it was special.

Deon, wearing a black tuxedo, was laughing and drinking champagne as well. They exchanged quick smiles.

Soft music played in the background, just a harp, flute, and guitar. The weather was perfect for December. No snow, and mild temperatures.

They hadn't cut the cake yet but David was full from a gourmet dinner. Deon made his way over with a group of his friends who flew in from Paris to be at their wedding.

Deon asked David, "What is veep?"

David laughed. "It's a nickname for vice president."

One of Deon's friends asked David, "So you are 'veep' when they speak of it?"

"Yes. I'm the Vice President. The 'veep'."

"Still very powerful." Deon hooked David's arm and finished his champagne.

"Next time you will be president. Yes?"

"I don't know. I'm very happy where I am." David hugged Deon with one arm and spotted his son.

Jim, his hair grown back finally, wore a suit and…was with a date. A young man.

When David smiled at him, Jim walked over, holding hands with his young friend and Deon noticed and moved back so Jim could join their circle. Deon did not, however, smile at Jim. David understood completely how Deon felt, and did not push them to make amends.

"Are you proud of your father?" one of Deon's friends asked Jim. "He is a veep!" he laughed.

"I am." Jim blushed and looked at the young man who was with him. "I think my dad should have been the president, but he said he wanted more time…to be with his family."

"I did." David set his empty glass down as a server walked by with a tray. Deon did as well.

"You are stepson of our Deon?" One of Deon's friends asked, playfully, nudging Jim.

Deon snarled slightly and picked up another full glass of champagne, as if he wanted no part of the conversation.

Jim shook his head. "That's way too weird now, ya know?"

David nudged Deon, hoping one day Deon could forgive, but David had struggled with that forgiveness as well. "Yes. It is. I know." David knew Deon's friend was just trying to be silly, but bringing up that old wound was a mistake. And David could easily sense Deon's distaste, which mirrored his own.

"Mind if I leave, Dad?" Jim asked. "Ian and I are going to a club and try to get a gig."

"You put in a good showing." David winked. "Get lost."

Jim kissed his father's cheek, then walked away.

"Don't look so angry." David nudged Deon and shook his head. "He has apologized many times to both of us."

"Is hard." Deon shrugged. "Some wounds too deep."

An announcement was made that it was time to cut the cake. David and Deon walked over to the many layered centerpiece and David warned Deon, "You smash it into my mouth and you will be sorry."

"Is undignified. For…veep." Deon held David's hand and they posed for photos as they cut a slice of the cake, complete with two tuxedo-clad grooms at the top.

Flashes of cameras went off, and David allowed Deon to feed him a bite. And Deon was polite and did not mess David up when he did.

David however, scooped up a huge portion on the fork and Deon could see what was coming. He began laughing and backing away, holding up his hand. David moved after him and finally Deon stood still and opened his mouth.

David didn't have the heart to do it, so he took a small piece between his fingers and fed it to Deon. Deon sucked on David's sweet fingertips and hoots and howls filled the small hall.

"*Merci*," Deon said as he finished swallowing. "I do detest that silliness."

"And besides." David kissed him. "How would it look from a man who is now a vice president, and a model that represents the largest diamond dealer in the world?"

"Like a power play, yes?" Deon held onto David and smiled as the photographer took more photos. "And you and I? We no need power any longer. We are simply two men."

"Two men in love." David held Deon tightly and kissed him again.

More shouts of encouragement and forks making tinkling noises hitting bell glasses rang out around them.

"Too the veep and his sheep!" Deon announced.

David roared with laughter and knew no one else was aware of the joke. He looked at the friends and family around him and yes, of course they invited supporters and loved ones, but heck, he was now the first Vice President, married to a man.

One baby step at a time.

And for David, marrying Deon, was a huge leap.

He swept Deon into his arms and said, "I think its time for the wedding night."

"Oh!" Deon blinked in surprise. "No more want to dance?"

"Nope." David began carrying him out of the hall.

"No more dessert?"

"I think I know what my dessert will be." The door was held open for David and a black limousine decorated with ribbons and flowers was waiting out front.

The media was there, having been kept out of the ceremony and reception after. David set Deon on his feet and held Deon's hand holding up the ring. He pointed to it. "Your veep is legally married. Say hello to the new second lady...I mean man, of the White House!"

He entered the back of the limousine as the media tried to throw questions at them, but they blocked them out and the limousine left.

"That will get the far right tongues wagging," David said, looking out of the rear window.

"I know where I want tongue to wag." Deon leaned against David.

David put his arm around him and they kissed.

David had no idea if his new man was going to be loved or mocked in the media, but he had no time for that...not any longer. He was happy. Yes. Happy. And the only power play David wanted was who was going to play the lion or the lamb...in bed.

Deon parted from the kiss and smiled.

"Are you going to be my lion, Deon Gael-Asher?"

"I will be yours, forever...lion or lamb, David Asher-Gael."

David laughed and held Deon's jaw, kissing him as they drove away from the hall, for a night of loving, in bed.

The End

About the Author

Award-winning author G.A. Hauser was born in Fair Lawn,
New Jersey, USA and attended university in New York
City. She moved to Seattle, Washington where she worked
as a patrol officer with the Seattle Police Department. In
early 2000 G.A. moved to Hertfordshire, England where
she began her writing in earnest and published her first
book, In the Shadow of Alexander. Now a full-time writer,
G.A. has written over 100 novels, including several best-
sellers of gay fiction. GA is also the Executive Producer for
her first feature film, CAPITAL GAMES and in the midst
of directing and post-production for her second film
NAKED DRAGON.
For more information on other books by G.A., visit the
author at her official website.
www.authorgahauser.com
www.capitalgamesthemovie.com
www.nakeddragonthemovie.com

The G.A. Hauser Collection

Single Titles

Unnecessary Roughness

Hot Rod

Mr. Right

Happy Endings

Down and Dirty

Lancelot in Love

Cowboy Blues

Midnight in London

Living Dangerously

The Last Hard Man

Taking Ryan

Born to be Wilde

The Adonis of WeHo

Boys

Band of Brothers

Rough Ride

I Love You I Hate You

Code Red

Marry Me

Timeless

POWER PLAY

The Farmer's Son

One Two Three

Three Wishes

COPS

Bedtime Stories

The Reunion

The Ugly Truth

Hardcore Houston

Lie With Me

I'd Kill For You

Aroused and Awakened

Power Play

Trent is a Slut

Four Men and a Funeral

L.A. Masquerade

Dude! Did You Just Bite Me?

My Best Friend's Boyfriend

The Diamond Stud

The Hard Way

Games Men Play

Born to Please

Got Men?

Heart of Steele

G. A. HAUSER

All Man

Julian

Black Leather Phoenix

London, Bloody, London

In The Dark and What Should Never Be

Mark and Sharon

A Man's Best Friend

It Takes a Man

Blind Ambition

For Love and Money

The Kiss

Naked Dragon

Secrets and Misdemeanors

Capital Games

Giving Up the Ghost

To Have and To Hostage

Love you, Loveday

The Boy Next Door

When Adam Met Jack

Exposure

The Vampire and the Man-eater

Murphy's Hero

Mark Antonious deMontford

214

POWER PLAY

Prince of Servitude

Calling Dr Love

The Rape of St. Peter

The Wedding Planner

Going Deep

Double Trouble

Pirates

Miller's Tale

Vampire Nights

Teacher's Pet

In the Shadow of Alexander

The Rise and Fall of the Sacred Band of Thebes

G. A. HAUSER

The Action Series

Acting Naughty

Playing Dirty

Getting it in the End

Behaving Badly

Dripping Hot

Packing Heat

Being Screwed

Something Sexy

Going Wild

Having it All!

Bending the Rules

Keeping it Up

Making Love

Staying Power

Saying Goodbye

Men in Motion Series

Mile High

Cruising

Driving Hard

Leather Boys

Heroes Series

Man to Man

Two In Two Out

Top Men

Wolf Shifter Series

Of Wolves and Men

The Order of Wolves

Among Wolves

G.A. Hauser
Writing as Amanda Winters

Sister Moonshine

Nothing Like Romance

Silent Reign

Butterfly Suicide

Mutley's Crew

CPSIA information can be obtained
at www.ICGtesting.com
Printed in the USA
LVHW080321100519
617377LV00013B/99/P